For:
A great friend and neighbor.
I hope the entire family enjoys
this story.
 Parmenter

SUNDOWN

Parmenter Welty

Copyright © 2023 John Parmenter Welty

Independently published.

All rights reserved. Except for use in critical reviews or works of scholarship, the reproduction or use of this work in any form, or by any electronic, mechanical, or other means now known or hereafter invented, including photocopying and recording, and in any information storage and retrieval system, is forbidden without written permission of the author. For permission requests, write to the publisher, addressed "Attention: Permissions Coordinator," at the email address below.

Names, other than of certain public figures referred to only, or places, other than New York City and other real U.S. states and countries, are products of the author's imagination. Any incidents, dialogues, or other persons used in the story bearing resemblance to actual events, dialogues, or persons, are entirely coincidental.

ISBN – 9798860300569
First printing edition 2023
parmenter.welty@gmail.com
editor: Liana Welty

To my wife Liana for her love, enthusiasm and assiduous editing of my books.

"Ad meliora. Ad astra per aspera."

Toward better things. Through adversity to the stars.

TABLE OF CONTENTS

Chapter 1	----------	page 1
Chapter 2	----------	page 27
Chapter 3	----------	page 62
Chapter 4	----------	page 91
Chapter 5	----------	page 117
Chapter 6	----------	page 145
People & Places	-----------	page 154

Chapter 1

Abigail Boone my name. Some folk thinks I a retard. Me, my mama Jasmine, an Big Mama (mama's mama) moved up to this northern town from Camel City, North Cackalacky – North Carolina that is – over a year ago, in summer 1954, after mama gots married ta Mr. Jones.

My boyfriend Tad'n I fifteen. One night we went ta watch a basketball game. That where my story begin.

Fwap! That empty coke bottle hit them floorboards like a bomb careenin from outer space, then bounce a little but dont break an skitter across the floor spinnin cattywampus hittin the ball the player on the other team was dribblin down the court. The referee man seen it an kicked it to the sidelines by sweepin it with his foot back in the direction it come from where we was sittin without even lookin in our direction. It werent the first thing throwed out there. Wadded-up papers an such was hittin the floor already litterin the oak boards an people fillin the air with chants an mean shouts "Nigger go home!" at them Negro boys on the out-a-town team yellin they shouldnt oughta come inta our town ta play basketball but "stay in the trees with the monkeys."

Before I gets confused and ahead a myself, I gots ta tell that thanks ta my neighbor Mrs. Wesley ya-all can read an understand what I writes – even these here words. It lots worse when I shows it ta Mrs. Wesley first off. I ask er bout the words I dont know how ta spell, but she weren't wantin ta correct it all right off, sayin she want me ta do what I can. Sos I gots ta pologize now for all my writin mistakes.

My boyfriend Tad gots real excited by all the carryin on an throwed that coke bottle, underhanded cuz he feared it might break an put a dent in the floor a the Protestant high school gymnasium. After it roll an break the dribble, folks behind slapped im on the shoulders congratulatin im. Nobody done nothin to im, just started laughin bout it. His real name Larry but everyone call im *Tadpole*. He gots kind of a chubby, baby face an his last name Lapierre. They razz him that when he growed up he gonna turn into a frog, but til then he still a tadpole. He splained his nickname ta me once, but I couldnt get it. I just calls im Tad.

The out-a-town team won the game anyways. Folks werent happy, some real mad, an I hears em say it werent fair ta let "the niggers" play gainst our team cuz they was all bred back in the day fer physical stuff, so they had the vantage. A big crowd went out ta the back a the school where the bus fer the outa-town team was parked, waitin fer em ta come out. It werent my first time ta see a basketball game in Glasstonburg. I knowed already how things was in that town. Cuz that team come from another town an had some negro boys on it, the bus park in the back.

Tad gots all worked up like them others. He drug me along ta see what the crowd would do. He got frustrated cuz nothin much different did, only more a the same name callin. The bus parked up real close ta the back door a the school. Two policemens there, one on each side the openin, sos when the players come out wid the door open, they jump inta the bus as fast as a mother hen pecks grain. Cuz the policemens blockin the crowd from gettin close, they start yellin that mean "N" word over an over, even when the bus start rollin away over the gravel. I never seen nothin like that in North Cackalacky. (Mrs. Wesley say I best not use that word, even though it the way we kids calls our state. She say that word "juvenile, a word used mostly by children.")

It not cuz I never heard that 'N' word fore, but I knows folk who uses it angry. At what, I dont know. If they thinks they bettern negro folk they uses it fer, then why aint they happy? Instead, they always angry when talkin bout colored folk, cept when makin jokes about em. I tell Tad that too, cuz it aint only at basketball games I hears that word in this town. Tad say I should shut up bout things I knows nothin bout, specially cuz a my nickname Nig. I tries ta make im explain what he mean but he dont say nothin.

***

Mrs. Wesley live cross the city-limit road. After her husband went ta the big city up over on the lakes ta work, she stayed put with their two kids. She dont work cuz er husband send money, so even fore I start cleanin er house once a week, she an me become good friends. I showed er my writin bout Mr. Jones farm we lives on an bout this town what seem so strange ta me. I wanna write about what I sees around me. She read it and sigh real heavy, then offer ta help straighten it out, correct spellin an lotsa other things so folks can understan what I sayin. I fixin ta put er coachin in brackets.

[She say whatever I wants ta say should be "faithful to your way of talking. Making it all standard English would be a pity."
"Spell correctly the short words first", she say, startin with 'and', 'to', 'into', 'for', 'of' and 'with', instead of 'an', 'ta', 'inta', 'fer' 'a' and 'wid'; Spell 'him', 'her' and 'them' instead a 'im', 'er' and 'em'," and some others she give me a list for next time I brings her new stuff to correct. She promise if I "stick to it" I can learn the right way ta write and talk and not stay "confused about grammar." But she say that if I stops usin "those colorful expressions from the Tarheel state," her helpin me would be as useful as tits on a bull. She dont talk that way, but that what she mean. She want to teach me how to make things I writes "understandable in the context."]

Like a bull snake what shuck off its old skin, one day maybe I be happy to see how I changed cuz I can see myself in a new way. It not real clear to me what I should keep and not keep, but I wants to get the grammar right. That almost as important to me as tellin what I wants to say.

First thing I remarked on livin in Glasstonburg was almost all kids in school gots nicknames. Soon after we come here, the kids started namin me "Nig". Back where we used to live, sometimes I gots called "Gabi" because my name Abigail Boone, so it just change my first name around to mean I talks a lot, which is true. I dont know why they calls me that new nickname here, but my schoolmates thinks it fit. Nobody never wanted to splain why they calls me that way. While layin down in the hay barn on the farm, in the private place we calls "the gallery" connected to tunnels my step brothers built deep under the piled up bales, one day my new girlfriend Ruth-Ann tell me.

"It doesn't mean a thing", she break out sayin first off.

"It gotta mean somethin," I answers back. She give me a serious kinda look, then promise to let it all out and tells me them others, but not her, thinks I talks funny, with a "southern accent," somethin like "the colored people", and that I's darker than the rest of the kids. She say they knows I werent no pickaninny, but I act strange, in ways kids in that town dont, chatter away about things most cant understand. "You seem a little slow too", she finish sayin in a soft whisper, lookin down with her eyes. Then she look up.

"But I just see you as different. Since most of the kids think you're "halfway in that direction," they say, they made up the nickname Nig to call you. But we all have nicknames, so it shouldn't bother you."

I say back I werent bothered, just wants to know how come they calls me that way. I stop talkin bout it and start goin along on all fours crawlin through them tunnels collectin ten eggs laid by the hens what went along that way too. It a good place to look for eggs.

Truth is, none of them kids knows any negro folks, so I has to wonder how come they thinks I talks like them. Back in North Cackalacky, Carolina that is, where I was born and raised up til us three come here, livin with Mr. Jones and his kids now, negro folks lived all round us but we didnt call them that mean word that way. They was our neighbors. Mama say my papa half Cherokee and some other neighbors of ours was Lumbee Indians. Mama is part Cherokee too but say she dont know how much or which part. There was plenty white folks in our town in North Carolina and some used that mean 'N' word, but only when them negro neighbors werent nearby.

Papa left us when I was still playin in the street. Maybe he didnt wanna be papa to more kids. Nowadays I wonders sometimes maybe he didnt wanna be papa to me or even didnt like me cause my eyes is blue-green. I dont look like him except for my dark skin and hair and I takes a long time to learn new things. He all the time got mad at me not learnin what he say should be easy, and never spent moren a look-see to help me with school lessons. Anyways, one day right after I turned seven, we didn't see him no more cept once in a while when we out and about. Mama know where he went and say he werent comin back. Turned out she right. She never looked for another man or give in to offers until Mr. Jones come along.

***

Mama met my new papa, Mr. Jones, not long fore they gots married. Mama say he "swept me off my feet", seemin to be in a big hurry to make her his wife. She was workin at the North Carolina State Fair where he went to learn more bout raisin tobacco. He was thinkin maybe he make more money if he planted it in his fields, but finally figured it werent hot long enough up in this northern state to raise a good crop and didnt know if he could find any helper livin round here who know how to cure it, so he dont plant none. Mostly he grow corn, soybeans and some hay too.

He own the house where we live, two other houses on the place he rent out to other families, all the rest of the sheds, barns and sawmill on the land and hundreds of acres he call a "small farm."

His first wife, who left him with five blond-haired kids all lookin like him, is in her grave. She musta been one of them better angels. I says that cause of the berry patch she started from baby plants that is now full of strawberries low down, thimbleberries thigh high, raspberries up higher, black and white currants on bigger bushes and some newcomers like blueberries and a blackberry bush what seem real healthy, each comin along with berries in its own time from late spring to early fall. She started raisin em in the ground on the way to where we digs up the taters from a mound on the edge of the field.

I likes thimbleberries, with their pretty white flowers, the way they peels off whole in your hand lookin like a thimble. Whenever we goes that way in late summer to get taters, we picks berries for the house fridge, and the Jones girls, who is old enough to remember their mama, talks about her, callin her "Mother Jones." The boys don't pick the berries, least not for the house, and I never hear them talk about their mama.

We calls Big Mama, mama's mama, "Elohi". I admits mama never insisted that her real name. I know it mean 'Earth' in Cherokee. Mr. Jones was glad to welcome her to his land, but bein' as how there no room for her in the house, he put up a trailer for her near to that berry patch. He gots all kind of equipment and with his loader shovel he dig a ditch for a water pipe to the trailer, puts a tank in the ground to drain the toilet, set up a propane drum nearby and gived Elohi a burner he hooked up so she could heat the place on the cold days.

Elohi bein raised in Oklahoma only come back to North Cackalacky when she gots married to a part white man, Mr. Boone, who was mama's papa, now dead. We thinks she gots mostly Cherokee blood in her cause of her looks, but she don't know and we ain't sure. It dont matter anyways cause she was raised on a reservation like as if she was. She speak what mama call "accented English." I don't even know if she can write it. She can talk Cherokee, but since I can't, we talks in English, sometimes about them berries what she call the "Mother Jones other children."

She an old woman now and wander all over the land behind her trailer pickin berries and other plants in summer. If we don't finds her inside the trailer, we usually finds her in the berry patch. She say she can feel the first Mrs. Jones mongst them berry bushes an say that woman's spirit happy there. I think Elohi talk to spirits we can't see, or at least I hears her talkin out loud in Cherokee when I finds her alone out there among the bushes. She tell me that the first Mrs. Jones welcome the blueberries and blackberries and believe their bushes come from seeds what is "cousins that made a long journey to be here." How she come to think that if she not talkin to the spirit of the first Mrs. Jones?

I like Big Mama cause she always smile at me and tell me I "a beautiful lady". She like to smoke weeds she find out near the berry patch what she roll up in papers. She hug me a lot which I has to admit I likes. Even if I knowed my other grandparents, she'd be my favorite.

***

The father of the first Mrs. Jones still live on the place in some rooms attached to one of them barns. I never got the invite to go inside, and I don't think he ever talk to Elohi. He an old man, a farmer like his own papa, got the farm from him and gived it to his daughter when she got Mr. Jones as a husband, who come from a farmin family too. Mr. Jones come to be owner of it all after she left this "vale of tears," my mama call it, but I never seen none of them Jones kids cry.

There barns on the farm where Mr. Jones keep hogs, two silos full of feed corn for them and a big muddy fenced-in yard with a pig-wallow and trees with shade where the hogs spend their days, cept in winter, and lots of chickens that roams all over. The chickens sleeps wherever they gets their puckers up to sleep, and lays eggs in the tool barns, tractor shed, places like under the harrow, next to rusty old plows what seem like they was maybe forgot and planted outside in the weeds to grow roots, around the fuel tank and pump, in the places where the hogs live, the saw-mill with the machinery and places where a person wouldnt likely expect. But their favorite place to leave eggs is in the big hay barn.

The hay barn a magic place. It where troubled kids forgets and plays together like the kids they is. My oldest stepbrother Jer climbed up once I don't know how to the rafters and tied a rope we use to swing out on before droppin down to the big pile of loose hay underneath. That the only place where we all laughs together, even me the oldest. There always hay stacked real high in bales, up close to the rafters in some places, and that where the Milk Brothers, my two oldest stepbrothers, worked weeks stackin them bales fore I come to live there, so now we gots tunnels to crawl through way down under near the bottom.

[Mrs. Wesley say I did good on that part, and give me a big hug, makin me real happy. She give me a bunch of lessons, sayin, "if you use this punctuation, and spell some other words right" in the next part, she gonna give me a big bowl of my favorite ice cream and a bigger hug. I just has to use the longer list she gived me and be careful].

The youngest Jones is a boy, now five, named Dennis, but we-all calls him "The Menace." The first Mrs. Jones died while he was bein born, so he have no memory of his mama. Up over him, the twin girls, Margie and Mercy, eight years old, was born together but dont look nothin alike except for havin blond hair. They gots nicknames too: "Knuckle" for Margie and "Brain" for Mercy. Both their nicknames was made up by their next older brother and he always talk to them together like they the same person: "Knuckle Brain" he always say. That boy come next in age. He twelve and his name no one use cept mama is Billie. He got the nickname "Moon Boy" cause he first choose the night of a big round one, what seemed as big as the Earth, fixin to start huntin rats by its light cause he figured he knowed where they was gatherin. The oldest boy, named Jerry, a year youngern me. We just calls him "Jer," but together we calls him and Moon Boy the "Milk Brothers," cuz as little babies Jer was still nursin and Moon Boy had to share his mama's tit with him.

None of them Jones kids calls me the same as kids in my school. They calls me "Gabi", the same way I got called in North Carolina. They say I always gabbin away like as if I wants the whole world to know I there and what I thinkin. I likes that name a whole lot moren Nig.

Some folks in town calls Mr. Jones "Sod," and I hears them call Jer and Moon Boy "Sons of Sod." So that way I knows some people gives diffent nicknames dependin on what they thinks is important and how they sees a person. In this town mama say some folks calls us "Tar Heels," in a mean way, cause we from North Carolina and they thinks the name mean we gots a little blackness to us like as if we got tar on our heels. I knows that aint what Tar Heel mean, so what they say cant be right lessen mama didnt understand, cause what she say dont make no sense.

Mama and me gots a visit one day after we been here only a coupla weeks from two ladies sayin they a "welcome wagon" to show us a greetin to the town. They brung us a lemon-meringue pie to give us and declared how much they preciated our bein new to town and asked Mama tons of questions about herself and me. I was thinkin they sure nosy but Mama acted real grateful.

"Why, bless your hearts!," she kept sayin, so I knowed right off she was playin pretend sweet, knowin that usin them words was like slappin them in their face.

After they wuz gone mama start stormin round the house maddern a wet hen. I couldnt figure out why, til she tells me, them two was both once wantin to hitch up with Mr. Jones and just come to spy on her. They wuz fixin to visit "out of jealous curiosity," mama say. "Besides," she tolded me, "that pie they brought was store bought. They didnt even bother to hide they didnt make it."

Mama dont use our made-up names, only our birth names Jerry, Billie, Margie, Mercy, Dennis, and Abigail, of course. She repeat many times,

"You kids can use any term you want for each other, but a parent who spent so much time deciding on a name for a child deserves to use that name." So, when she want to scole one of us, after callin that kid by the real name, she say, "I'm gittin that switch!" if someone was bad, and all them kids except Jer do what she want. She say there no reason to talk that way to Jer cause he almost a man now and cant be controlled. Cept once she say to him, "Now Jerry, tell me what you said one more time!" after hed mouthed back at her. He just look in her eye and dont say nothin more. That seem like all she need to say, cause now he most polite with her.

Mr. Jones and his children is Catholic. Jer goes to the Catholic high school and Moon Boy, Knuckle and Brain all goes to what they calls the "parochial school." The Menace is too young yet for school. I never talked bout people they dont know with the Jones kids, and I never hear that ugly 'N' word comin out their mouths. They don't go to watch basketball games at the Protestant high school, so maybe they dont even know colored folk exist.

My boyfriend Tad and me broke up after that basketball game when he throwed the coke bottle. He wuz all excited about bein slapped on the back, folks congratulatin him, and gots the notion he a real man of a sudden and tried to mash me. He wuz my boyfriend and all, but I dont like him tuggin me into the bushes when we walkin to his house and tryin to pull my skirt up. Sos I slaps him in the face to knock him out of his boy craziness, and pulls away from him, startin to run out of that hidin place. He just yell after me, sayin I werent worth it anyways and should be glad he even my boyfriend, then yell he dont like me no more, like as if he thought maybe the sun come up just to hear him crow. Nowadays I just tryin to do my chores and write bout my life here. He dont ever come round no more. If he do, I dont know what I might say to him, but it wont be to make up.

[Mrs. Wesley looked happy enough with that part, but the lessons and new lists of words to spell right sure gettin long. She teached me how "to avoid double negatives," and show me a mountain of contractions, reminding me what they are, where to put an apostrophe to replace a missing letter, and where one word should be two (like 'kind of' instead of 'kinda'), the difference between 'what' and 'that', which I mix up, and about the word 'them' and where not to use it ('the boys' and not 'them boys', for example). She say the real important stuff about what she call "ing words" and "present tense verbs" was comin' up later].

***

It do seem, like some folks says sometimes, that bad things comes together in threes. Not long after breakin up with Tad, which weren't one of the three bad things, for me anyways, right away come the first bad and sad thing that happened. The farm felt like it was my home by then, thanks partly to lovin to play in the hay barn. On that Sunday I was sittin on the slope in front of the back door of the house peelin taters from what we dug out the field near to Elohi's trailer to boil and soften up later to mash for dinner that evenin. I was just gazin out across the lower flat ground where one of the renter families keep huntin dogs tied up in front of dog houses set up partway round the edge of that open patch that sometime get flooded after a big rain.

I seen The Menace come barrelin down through the bushes that was on the slope between that low ground and the hay barn. He was only five but somethin sure make him run fast on his chubby little legs. I look back towards the hay barn, behind where he wuz runnin from, and seen a lick of yella near the openin we use to get into the barn.

The Menace come tearin up the slope and run into the house faster than I could get the peel loose from the tater. Mama come out with him in her arms and we wuz all three starin at the hay barn yonder. It was full on fire, flames pourin out all the open spaces and reachin up to the rafters. Other folks seen it too. Before I knowed it all them Jones kids and almost all our renter neighbors was gawkin at that fire. In just a couple of minutes it turn the whole big barn into a roarin blaze. Nobody even moved. Mama say later we wuz all "hypnotized by the sight of those awful flames licking up towards the sky," and we-all understood it was no use callin for a fire truck that couldn't get close enough to do any good anyways.

After only about thirty minutes the barn was gone, a giant smokin pile of burnt up rafters with sputterin flames here and there, 2x4s, siding boards and what-not, but not a twig of straw left. I never feeld so bad in my life cause the hay barn wuz gone.

"It appears all the shingles got consumed by the flames," Mr. Jones say later.

After the fire, mama took charge of The Menace. She don't yell or threaten him, like she might do with Knuckle or Brain, but start first by settin him on her lap, givin him a hug sayin,

"You were a brave little man to escape that fire all by yourself. We sure are glad, Dennis, that you knew to run and leave those matches." Mama don't know if he gots matches. She wuz just fishin. He keep his mouth shut, sayin nothin, so mama say they got a secret if he tell her where the matches come from. He looked up into her eyes. She smiled down at him, tryin to make him feel protected and comfortable. He tell her he found them in the sittin room.

"Where were they in the living room?", mama ask. He tell her they was in a drawer. Mama knowed from those words that Dennis stole the matches from where Mr. Jones smoke his pipe after dinner. She never had to ask anythin more.

While watchin mama get those words from The Menace, I wuz thinkin bout the hens in the hay barn that got caught in the fire and felt relieved and blessed that none of us others was in the tunnels. The Menace proved to everyone that day why he called "The Menace." To my thinkin, what he done was worse than anythin ever done by Dennis the Menace in the comics.

The second bad thing wuz Elohi died. After we found her, I cried all day and stayed home from school more than one. I was goin on sixteen and she wuz 62 or 63, mama figured. If she was sick, nobody knowed about it. Elohi never talk much but liked to listen to me gab about this and that, things happenin at school or to the Jones kids, always listenin with a smile.

I think she happy when she died because of how we found her. She weren't in the trailer, instead wuz in the middle of the berry patch with a bunch of berry plant leaves laid out in a big ring around her, includin from the huckleberry and blackberry bushes. Some had tiny green berries already. She was sittin with her head droppin forward in a sit-down position with her legs crossed, not layin down, wearin a dress we never seen on her before. Her face showed the biggest smile I ever seen on her.

I was with Knuckle and Brain and at first wonderd what she doin sittin there like that. When I lean in and touch her, I seen the truth, scream and start bawlin. Tears jumped off my face startin to run down my cheeks. I kissed her hair and forehead while sobbin away with my arms wraped around her neck. The berry bushes maybe like the tears I left on the ground, cept for the salt in them. Nowadays I dreams from time to time about Big Mama. She always wearin that same smile in those dreams. Rememberin how her face looked that day help me get to sleep.

Mr. Jones told Jer to use the "front-end loader" and scrape the blackberry bush out of there but to "be careful not to damage the others." Maybe he want to keep the berry patch his first wife start, or maybe he thinkin more about the berries because they make good desserts, but he knowed the blackberries would take over if not dug out. He say they weren't cousins to the other berries, like Elohi think.

Now, I gots to tell the third and last bad thing what happened. I was sort of waitin for a miracle to make me be smart, but I never got the hang of grammar in school, spellin, writin long pretty words, or algebra because I can't understand where the X comes from.
I sure likes to talk though. I can't wait to share ideas I thinkin about out loud in classes with them other kids. Our teachers was always scoldin me.
A day or two before the school year end, the principle and his assistant comes to me sayin the teachers couldn't help me anymore and I should "take advantage of the opportunity to leave for good at the end of the year, now that you are sixteen." Leavin school can't hurt me any way that I knows about. The other kids keeps callin me that nickname they give me that I don't like anyways and always hurt when I hear it, once I knowed they wuz makin fun of me. I gots other ideas about how to use my time anyhow.
Mama was sad for me but glad to get more of my help with the housework. Mr. Jones say he happy to see me bein a "back-up" for mama. We worked out a schedule that allow me time to write stuff, go to Mrs. Wesley twice every week, show her my scribbles, correct them, and give more lessons.

I don't understand why I wants to write about things or what might come out of it, but Mrs. Wesley say "my will and memory," bein so strong as they is, with my "gift of gab," I just needs to be "coached properly to learn grammar" to write better, "since you seem so keen to share your thoughts." Mrs. Wesley's puckers up for sure to work with me on my grammar and writin. I never knowed a person so kind and generous.

A boy got kicked out of our school a couple of years before me. It was more like an order than an invitation like they gived me. Two men from the school office put him in a car, drove to his house at the end of the school day after he turn sixteen and tole his mama they can't do nothin with him since he don't learn nothin. He nineteen now and some says he live in a shack in the city dump across the city-line road. A person standin on top of the hill on our farm can see the dump ground across a lower field of corn that belong to Mr. Jones.

That boy in the dump gots a nickname too. They calls him "Gyro Gearloose", maybe because he can fix gears on a bicycle or anythin metal that turns. Anyway, he gots a shack there he built where some says he live, but I don't know for sure. I don't see any way he can cook food there. And I don't know where he eat, sleep or stay warm when it get cold. For sure he not livin in high cotton there in the dump, but he don't seem to mind cause he love to collect and fix broken stuff so that it work right.

One time I went there with Mr. Jones and seen him. I says to him, "Hi y'all, Gyro!" He tell me back, kinda shy like, that his real name Patrick. He tell me I might oughta come back and see him. I answers I might could.

I never went back, but from us chattin I knows we alike because he don't like people givin him a nickname to call him that he don't like and that nobody even ask him if he like bein called that way.

    I gots one more thing to say about that cornfield we can look across and see the city dump ground from. Around here, it rain lots in late Fall and the ground, bein mostly clay, hold the water. It stay put and freeze over so we gots a large lake to skate on come winter. We races off down there on the frozen ground and spends lots of time playin on the ice. I pulls on my figure skates, tries goin in circles and doin pirouettes, leavin me most times on my butt, but real happy anyways. The boys plays hockey with sticks and a rock. The ice stay so long sometime we think it gonna be there forever.

    The first March we lives there, I was skatin alone and falls through the ice. Instead of landin in the water, I drop more than two feet and land in the mud that covered my skate runners. Real surprised and a little scared, I hunker down low anyways sos I can look far away under the ice. There was no water as far as I see because by March it all drained away. The field have bumps and hollows. The bumps holds up the ice where the ground touches it. Where I fell through was a deep hollow space. I remember thinkin how I spected one thing but found another I didn't spect. The ice was rotten. How much rotten ice do it take to cover over the truth about what underneath?

    [Mrs. Wesley is gettin real serious now. She show me how to write what she call "comparatives" ('more than', not 'moren', for example), and give me a list of words she say I "always write without the first letters." Once she sure I can tell a verb from a noun, she show me examples on every page of the same mistake. "Verbs that should end in 'ing', you always write without the 'g', like 'gettin' when it should be 'getting'. She show how I do the same way with nouns that end in 'ing'. We see enough examples so I understand.

"Now I want you to write the final 'g'." I say I can try but know I won't always get it right.

For the first time she gives me lessons about verbs: how to use and spell 'is', 'am', 'are' in the present and 'were' and 'was' in the past.

I have to remember to write 's' at the end of a present tense verb for it', 'he' and 'she', and none for all other persons. I always do it opposite. The clue is always to remember who or what does the doing. If the doer is more than one, the verb takes no 's', most usually.

For the past tense verbs, I usually guess or don't use them. Mrs. Wesley spends time now teaching me the past tense verbs. I believe I am getting the idea for the first time. After a ton of lessons, she's turning me loose. I got lots more to write about].

***

Moon Boy is now a rambling teenager hunting rats all over the farm. His grandpapa not long back made him an offer that got him and Long Jon partnered up. I'm going to try to tell it the way they told me. One day, his grandpapa buttonholes that young rascal and promises to give him an Indian head nickel for every rat he can show him dead. Naturally, he was interested. He got his puckers up to get some coins in his pocket for practicing what he loves doin anyways. By that time Moon Boy killed lots of rats but just leaves them in the weeds. He can't show he killed them and anyways by that time they were just dried skin. He leaves them where they can't be found any more, so his grandpapa's offer is good starting only on that day when he shows him a brand-new dead rat.

Moon Boy starts hunting night and day. He sets up muskrat traps in barns where he knowed they run through. He ties the traps to jute strings and shoves them real deep and slow with a long stick into narrow spaces so they won't spring closed by accident. Then he waits outside. Not long after, he hears the trap snapping shut. He don't even have to use bait because the rats just run over it and the set trap does the rest. He yanks on the string, pulling the trap and rat outside where he is sittin in the sunshine, saying to himself – "That's a nickel!" There were times the rat weren't dead and he kills it by choppin off its head. Yuk! I cringe when he tells me the story.

That worked for a time. But after he gets some bodies, the traps stop snapping shut. He listens but can't get more rats that way. He tells me he thinks the rats come to understand they have to jump over or go around the traps. He thinks maybe they smell his touch on the metal and even starts to half-believe they pass on what they learn between themselves. One way or another, the rats was smarter than he thought.

He weren't making much money but then got Long Jon, Mrs. Wesley's boy from across the road, as his partner to come up with better ideas. Long Jon is a couple years older than Moon Boy but just as keen to kill rats.

They decide to try a different way. First, they get some old wood handles like broomsticks. When a broom or something else is attached to the end of some, they cut it off with a saw. Then they get some big nails from Mr. Jones sawmill and hammer one partway into the end of each of the sticks, cut off the heads and file down the part sticking out, turning the sticks into spears with long points. That way, they have a couple of spears between them. They were going out at night. Long Jon argues they might oughta paint charcoal over their faces, but finally they just set out one night of a full moon with their spears and white faces and traipses out to the main chicken coop set at the top of that big cornfield part way in the direction of the city dump.

Some chickens go in there at night, even though they can wander all over the farm, because troughs sit in there that me and the Jones girls, for our newest chore, are fixin to keep full of feed grain all the time. (I can't believe 'trough' is spelled that way).

Mr. Jones has a plan to attract more hens to that coop since the hay barn burnt down. They can't go there anymore anyway. He hopes to get them all to live there and lay eggs in that one place so me and the girls only has to go to that one place to look for eggs instead of in other buildings, tall grass, under abandoned plows, and such.

Down a long slope and way across the bottom of that cornfield that floods from rain in the fall, then freezes in winter like I wrote about, is the city dump. Rats in the dump come to explore that chicken house up on the hill across that corn field not long after Mr. Jones set the coop out there. If Moon Boy is right that rats spread information to the others, that explains why that chicken house by itself out in the field attracts so many. It was better for them than eating corn through a picket fence.

Living in tunnels they dug by then under that chicken coop for sure must've made them feel finer than a frog hair split four ways, finer than a well-fed fish with no predators, because all they has to do is jump up through holes they chewed in the floorboards to fill their bellies on the feed we-all leave in there that supposed to be for the hens.

But Moon Boy and Long Jon was about to change all that by becomin predators. Steppin quietly through the doorway into the coop, moonlight shows clear as daylight three black rat profiles against the pale color of the chicken feed, eating their fill. Both boys throw their spears. One rat jumps away and disappears in the dark. The other broomstick spear lands in the feed trough and starts waving around in the air. The third rat waits long enough for Long Jon to throw the other spear he was holding and pins that rat to the wood after running it through the neck. Both Long Jon and Moon Boy speared a rat! I believe them telling me how excited they were, runnin out into the moonlight with the rats danglin from the spear points. The moon was bright, and like wild savages they hanged the bodies "in effigy," they say, and declared death to all rats, dancing like loonies in the moonlight. That was the real beginning of the rat wars.

The rat wars started about a month ago and they still goin strong. I ask Moon Boy to tell me all the latest news about it as it happens and he is more than happy to oblige. The two boys tried the spears at night again a couple of times but got only one rat dead to show grandpapa.

Long Jon got lots more ideas. They both have 22-rifles and start going out to that chicken house in daytime. Stretched out on the ground alongside each other, they park the rifle ends on a big beam that holds the chicken house off the ground about 18 inches so they can see underneath where the ground was full of holes. They got what they call "ringside seats", just layin there watching the rats come and go, some climbin, some jumpin, to get into the coop.

Moon Boy says with their 22s they changed the scene "into a shooting gallery, like at the county fair". "Long Jon's rifle is only a single shot", Moon Boy says, so he has to reload each time and only killed two rats while Moon Boy brags he picked off five during the same time. The seven rat bodies have to be pulled out and that weren't easy. After going around the chicken house, they find an opening they can crawl through and decide it was only fair for each boy to pull out the same number he killed. They come back to the house covered in dirt, prouder than a cock-a-doodle-doo rooster struttin around a barnyard of hens.

Jer, Moon Boy's older brother, and another boy we call "Uncle", were soon fixin to join in the war, because both Moon Boy and Long Jon have long tongues when talking and can't keep secrets any more than a flea sneezes.

They're "loaded for bear", their grandpapa declares, proud of himself for being the cause of the rat wars from the start. Whenever around his two grandsons he sticks his hands into his front pockets and shakes them so the boys can hear his change jingling and tells them he is waiting to pay for more dead rats.

With all four boys chasing after rats, the rat wars become a whole lot more ambitious. They pull apart old wood piles, pick up big boards and plywood sheets laying in the weeds and set more muskrat traps along the runs in all the barns, but don't kill enough to make it worth more than a fart in a rain barrel. They got only three of them dead with hatchets while the rats were scurryin away from under the wood, but only by stroke of luck. Seems like it's getting harder to find and kill more rats.

By then, though, they don't care about the nickels. For boys their ages it was the urge to kill that was driving them on. They turned downright savage. The last report I hear was the most disgusting one so far. All four of those boys have a 22-rifle and they're takin to using them mostly. Sitting against the wall of a hog pen at their backs, each with his rifle ready, facing towards a short half wall in the direction of the part of the farm that runs downhill towards yonder woods across another corn field, they was waitin together one morning.

A rat starts walking across the top of the low wall less than six feet in front of them. In their minds, they were in the shootin gallery again, and all four rifles raise up and fire. The rat falls to the other side. Quick as a cottonmouth strikes, Moon Boy has the rat in his hand. But it weren't dead. He pulls out a firecracker left over from the July celebration, sticks it up the rat's rear hole and Uncle lights the match after Moon Boy puts it back on the ground. Now, I don't want to know any more about those awful, nasty rat wars.

Chapter 2

"I think I've been missing the point about you," Mrs. Wesley said one day after my 17th birthday, "like looking at the trees, and not seeing the forest." Then she explained what she meant. I said I was learning a lot from her and wasn't that the point?

"We hear all the time in the news about Sputnik and how this country has to catch up with the Russians. What do you think about that, Abigail?" I didn't need time to answer, saying right off that if people just thought about improving themselves instead of all the time comparing themselves to others the world would be better off.

At first, she looked at me funny-like, followed by a smile that grew on her face. She reached over and gave me a long hug, and said she now had no doubt. "It is clear to me that you think more about things than I ever suspected." I thought she was changin the subject when she said next,

"You have excellent recall, Abigail. You always repeat almost exactly what you hear, but when you paraphrase you go back to using your own vernacular. That is very odd, because you generally show by what you say that you understand. Since your speech has become much more like standard English, I no longer doubt that you can learn maybe even better than lots of others.

"You are studying grammar, spelling, and word choice, but I am studying you. You are not simple at all, but very complex. I have understood for some time that you listen almost exclusively to yourself, while silently taking in a great deal of understanding. I believe that your intense drive to write is a way to release thoughts – of getting out of yourself, because for you talking is not enough. It's like you invented your own way to get out of your vernacular prison."

I partly got what she was talking about. But Mrs. Wesley wasn't finished yet.

"Having these ideas about you helps me help you. I agree with you: you have made great progress, and making progress is the point. I propose we retain what we have been doing together but add in different activities to pull the outside world into your consciousness so that it can enlarge".

I understood what she said in the beginning, but she lost me with her last words. By then, though, I believed she knew the best way for me. Starting that day we read passages to each other from newspapers and novels, like *The Yearling* by Marjorie Kinnan Rawlings and some others, and I had to repeat it as best as I could. Talking about it, she made me use words from the text. That way, I realized my reading was getting better. She still says she is "hesitant to smother your original voice," but I am just happy to see I'm improving. I used to think I was just stupid.

[Lessons take longer now with reading added to the grammar and spelling. Verbs are more complicated than what she told me before. "Auxiliary verbs", she explained, make it so even 'he', 'she' and 'it' don't take an 's' at the end: for example, 'He could eat', 'can eat', or 'did eat' is another way to write 'he eats' without using an 's'.

Mrs. Wesley is always reminding me of the rules to spell what she calls regular verbs. "Everybody must memorize the spelling of the irregular ones", she says, and gave me a longer list to study. I am excited. Everything is getting a lot clearer].

***

Mrs. Wesley rents part of the house across from ours on the city-limit road that runs far out into the country after passing over the railroad tracks. The owner's son and wife live upstairs and she, her daughter Pamela, called Pam, and boy Jonathan, called Long Jon on account of bein short, live downstairs. Pam is ten and Long Jon sixteen, a year younger than me.

Mama calls their driveway a "drive-through" because a driver <u>can</u> turn into it from Trench Road, go past the front of the house, turn right passing the garage and go out to city-limit road. (The word '<u>can</u>' is a good example of an auxiliary verb that works with all the verbs that follow not take an 's' at the end when the subject is 'he', 'she' of 'it'. That shows how much I am learning).

Our house across the road is on higher ground. We gaze down at the Wesley house. It's big, kind of run-down lookin, but sort of like the idea was once to make it grand with wagon wheels planted at the corners of the giant grass yard. Our place is smaller, even though we got more people livin here. Stairs go up to a bedroom in the attic under the roof, decorated pretty by mama, where she and Mr. Jones sleep. In the basement are two bedrooms for us kids.

The basement in the Wesley house has only a coal bin and furnace where Long Jon has the chore to shovel chunks of coal from the bin into what he calls "the hopper".

I got my own bed in the biggest room in our basement, which I share with Knuckle and Brain who sleep in their own bed together. The second bedroom has a three-level bunk where The Menace sleeps on the bottom, Jer in the middle and Moon Boy up on top. When The Menace turned four after me and mama moved in, Mr. Jones made him sleep in that room where he built a third level to the bunk. Mama told Mr. Jones she doesn't want the little boy to have to climb up top to sleep. He tosses around and could fall off. The Milk Brothers flipped a coin and Moon Boy got the top bunk. That was lucky, because he sleeps like a bird on a wire, never moving to peep or pee once asleep.

***

Behind Mrs. Wesley's house is where the Southside really starts. It doesn't look like the northern part of town because houses on the Southside look no better than Dogpatch shacks.

Long Jon's buddy Ronnie we call Uncle (one of the partners in the rat wars), for being the real uncle of another boy a year and a half older than him, lives further up Trench Road. The house Uncle lives in with two sisters and his mama and papa, has a dirt floor with chickens running in and out, sometimes walking on the kitchen table when the weather is warm, because the screen door doesn't close all the way, Long Jon tells me. And there is a toilet lyin in the dirt on its side in the front yard. The outhouse behind the house has no toilet.

Me and Long Jon walked up that way the other day. He showed me the place so I could see it with my own eyes. The front yard has garbage and stuff lyin around, and there is no grass. In North Carolina I never seen folks livin like that.

Pam, the little sister of Long Jon, gets picked up each day by a school bus and rides to school on the west side of town.

"That school, where they make all the kids on the Southside go, should be condemned," Long Jon tells me. "it's so old. In the schoolyard there's a shed left over from when it was the boys' outhouse. That's how out-of-date it is – a relic from the past." But for a boy who once went to such a poor, old school, he sure is smart. I wish I was smarter, but thanks to my list I'm spelling many words the way they are supposed to be spelled instead of how they sound in my head and I'm reading a lot better. I like Mrs. Wesley's lessons because I see I can learn from them.

Several months went by since I last showed Mrs. Wesley my writing. Even though I am still studying with her, I feel funny showing what I write. Now that I'm eighteen, I don't know if it is because I am older, or because I understand grammar a lot better, but I feel shy showing my imperfect writing. I just hope this feeling will pass, because now the Wesleys are my best friends.

The reading we do together has for sure made my vocabulary grow bigger. Now that I have more words, I want to be more like her to please her.

There is so much to learn. Sometimes that makes me feel worse than before, knowin I have so much more to learn. But I try not to be discouraged. I decided to keep a dictionary by my side when I write. Now that I'm learnin how to use it, it has become a habit.

Before movin on with my story and changes in my life, I want to say a little more about my stepbrothers, the Milk Brothers. Jer's a lot more serious than Moon Boy. He sure surprised me when he announced out of the blue to us other kids at the dinner table one night when he was still sixteen that he was fixin to go to Long Island in New York to a special camp for boys thinking about becoming priests.

Jer was gone sooner than we-all suspected. He didn't write us much that I know about, but after summer he was back with stories about how he discovered being a priest weren't what he wanted to do in life, though he knew he didn't want to be a farmer. He liked the summer camp though, he said, where they had lots of fun.

One story he told still sticks with me about playin a game he called "leap-frog" over there lots of times with the "brothers", his word for the priests. They hopped over each other in a line with their legs stretched out sideways while taking turns jumping, using their hands for support on the boy's back in front who was bent forward with his head down. The last in line was always the next to jump 'til he got to the front. The line always moved towards the salt water in the bay that was at the edge of the camp.

Since there were almost as many brothers as boys, it weren't unusual for one of the Catholic brothers to leap-frog over a boy in his priest clothes and land in the water. That was the beginning of the real fun, he told us, when everyone went in the bay for a swim. Jer didn't share much more than that, but I could tell he had serious thoughts in his head about what he wanted to do with his life. He never talks to me much, not seeming to have anything he wants to share, but I can tell he is always thinkin about his serious plans.

Moon Boy is a different kind. I can't ever think of him wanting to be a priest. I'm sure he'll be running the farm when he gets older. He talks mostly about obscene stuff, in a silly way, as if that's all he ever thinks about: maybe because he's a farm boy; but so is Jer, so I don't know. Only a couple of days after we moved up from North Carolina, he whispered he had something to show me. We snuck into the bedroom where only him and Jer were sleeping before The Menace was added to the room, and he showed me Jer's underpants. They were regular short white ones, not like boxer shorts, and they all had holes in the seats. Looking at me with his silly grin, Moon Boy started laughing, saying,

"See, Jer's a fart holder! He's always afraid someone will smell his farts, so he holds 'em in until he's alone and blasts a hole right through his shorts." I laughed at those words. Moon Boy was laughing too but I could see he meant all of it. I didn't expect that information, true or not, about his brother Jer, who I had only just met and never talked to him before or much after. I think Moon Boy's words told me more about him than about Jer. I suspected Moon Boy always wanted to embarrass me about personal stuff like that with jokes and songs with nasty bad words in them. Sure enough, without announcing beforehand, he once started right off singing this song to me:

Took my gal to the ball game,
Sat up near the fence.
Along came a fly ball
That hit her in the coun...

try boy, country boy,
Sittin' on a rock,
A bumble bee come flyin' by
And stung him on the co...

cktail, ginger ale...

I giggled, acted embarrassed and pushed him away before he finished, telling him to shut up. The song was funnier and didn't have language as rough as lots others I'd heard back in North Carolina, but by that time I was fourteen and felt more private and personal about that kind of thing, so I didn't want to hear his foul talk.

The last time he used his advantage with me, he asked in a serious voice if I wanted to hear a limerick. Not knowin what a limerick was, to explain he said it was a poem he learned at school (which weren't true: some friends of Jer's told it to him when he was waitin in their school for Jer). So, he fooled me into wanting to hear it. In a real loud voice, he started sayin,

"There was a young lady named Alice,
Who used TNT for a phallus..."

"What's a phallus? ", I asked. When he told me I slapped him real hard, telling him never to trick me again with his songs, poems and stories if they were jokes about obscene things with nasty words in them.

One thing he showed me was kind of cute, though, mainly because it had no obscene words in it. It was typed on a bar napkin with printed pictures and went like this:

There are only two things to worry about – either you're sick or you're well. If you're well, there's nothin to worry about. If you're sick, you got only two things to worry about – either you get well or you don't. If you get well, you got nothin to worry about. If you don't, you got only two things to worry about – either you live or you die. If you live you got nothin to worry about. If you die you got only two things to worry about – either you go to heaven or to hell. If you go to heaven you got nothin to worry about. If you go to hell, you're so busy shakin hands with all your friends you ain't got time to worry.

***

Mrs. Wesley tells me she and her husband got a legal separation recently. He still sends her money, but she doesn't know how much longer she can stay in this town and may have to leave sometime and take Long Jon and Pam to live with her folks in New York state because her husband started to talk about getting a divorce. She knows he has another woman but doesn't want to talk about it. To show she didn't need to depend on her husband anymore, she started a job as librarian in the big town nearby called Yankton City.

Shortly after hearing that news, I also found a full-time job in Glasstonburg. I'm now working behind the counter in 'Pauli's Soda Fountain and Ice-Cream Parlor' on the town square mixing up milk shakes, malts, ice-cream sundaes and things like that in my nice, white soda-fountain skirt uniform with a cute white and red striped top and cap for the town folk who come in and sit at the stools that run along the other side of the counter.

I like my job. It allows me to work my tongue full-time with the teenagers from school who come in to sit and make jokes while slurpin on their milk shakes. But I tell them right away to call me 'Abigail' or 'Gabi' like I'm used to on the farm. Some of those kids knew me as 'Nig', but I tell them not to use that name for me. With no teachers watching us, they're all free to talk to me and I'm learning lots of things I never knew about them before. Mabel (who most call 'Old Maid', usually behind her back, except for the meanest boys) comes in for ice cream too often for her figure, but I like to chat with her. Some boys gave her that nickname because they think she's homely, but I think she is a very nice person. Too bad for those boys who don't see her quality.

With so many folks crowding in most days I can't help but pick up on what's happening in the world. In the window of the parlor, we got magazines that tell about current events with photographs and pictures. I was surprised to see how many folks were interested to read about Elvis going into the army.

For the last little while everyone seated at the counter wants to talk about Elvis being drafted. I thought mostly the greaser boys who dress with pegged jeans, skinny belts and sometimes wear white shirts unbuttoned down to their belly buttons and wear their hair in a ducktail at the back with the special wave to the front part that hangs over, was mostly interested, but it seems everybody has something to say about Elvis. My stepbrothers get their hair made short in a crew-cut or flat-top but talk about him too.

'Possum' comes in sometimes. He was one of those boys who seemed to get the most kick out of calling me Nig. Of course, that is not his real name, which I don't even know. I wish I did so I could learn if he approves of the nickname they call him. Maybe only his family knows his real name, but in his case, it's most likely how he got that name. He looks like a possum. The hair on his head is naturally thin and sparse, I guess you'd say, and grey – even though he is my age. His face is long and rounded, comin to a point like the face of that animal, and it wouldn't take much to imagine him with whiskers sticking out from his cheeks. To us girls, he's so ugly and short, even shorter than Long Jon, some think he's almost cute, but not enough like a teddy bear for me to like. To me, he looks like he got whopped not only by the ugly stick but by the whole forest. He doesn't talk much when he comes in and he always seems glum.

I don't know much about it, but back when I was still in school, Possum was known to be the best, and fastest, dribbler of everyone and played on the high-school basketball team, even though he was so short, because once he had the ball nobody could catch him or get the ball. He always got it down the court to where he passed it to another player who was closest to shoot it in the basket. The coaches said at the time that he was "invaluable." It was almost like Possum kept a map of the other players in his head as they moved down the court and those boys he passed to didn't always expect it. His eyes seem a little further back on his head so maybe he could see more than the others. Some think he's not human, and everyone thinks he's a mystery.

 I hate to use a word like greaser for my new boyfriend Clifford Drum, but he wears his hair and sometimes dresses like one. Clifford is a very nice boy and real cute. Before I ever talked to him, he always come into the soda fountain shop with two or three other boys who wear their hair the same way he does. Usually, they sat in a booth and made boy talk that was too loud, looked over at me a lot, and laughed. One day, Clifford surprised me when he walked up to the counter and started talking to me real sweet and friendly. He said he knew I was a friend of Long Jon's who lives not far from him on the Southside and that Long Jon was once in his house to hear his papa play his electric dobro that he strums and plucks like a steel guitar on his lap. His papa's name is Langford. Clifford says his papa "performs solo, playin the fairs and events where he promotes himself as 'Drum and Dobro'".

 "Papa thinks that's a funny joke," he said. Those words make it sound like there is a drum in his music act, which there weren't.

 Cliff says his own nickname is just that short version of Clifford and I could call him by his short name. Right away he understood why I got called Gabi. He started coming into the shop more often after that. He told me a couple of the other boys who used to come in with him were always trying to make him talk to me. It took Cliff a couple more seconds to choose his words.

Finally, he said, "they knew I had a crush on you." After he said that, I understood why he felt shy telling me, because I felt shy then too. He's my boyfriend now – and he's much nicer to me than Tad ever was.

Working at Pauli's ice-cream parlor is fun and pleases me but I learn things here that are not so pleasing. I hear stories about this town that trouble me. More than one person told me pretty much the same story about a man who used to live right here on this square in a nice apartment. He was friendly and respectful to everyone and knew almost all folks. They admired him but didn't know much about him, where he come from and nothing about the other members of his family. He come as a young man, dated some women over time, but never married. Most everyone when strollin in town evenings greeted him because his daily habit was to walk around the four sides of the square after work dressed like for Sunday church with a cane in his hand.

He started working in the biggest factory in town right after he got here. He was smart, too, and his bosses come to recognize he had superior abilities. Over the years he got into administration and climbed the ladder, as folks say. After eighteen years or so he became the big boss, what they call the CEO, a job he kept for more than another fifteen years until he had to go to the hospital where he up and died of water on the brain, or something like that.

People in the town give him a funeral right away. Hundreds of folks attended, and they lined up to view him in his casket (which before I would have called a 'coffin'). The mayor and others in town tried to find out where he come from. That took some doin, but they finally did track his origin back to another town some couple hundred miles away. They wanted to get him back to his home and family so they could grieve and bury him proper with his family. A group of important people went with the hearse in two cars to deliver his body. They knew his last name was Niles, and that way tracked him back. When the group of people got to the address of his sister in that town and met her, they were the most shocked people on the planet.

She was a negro. Their friend Mr. Niles, an important member of the community, was what they called "a passer". Members of the group carried the casket inside, as polite as they could manage and left without further formalities. There was nothing else in the story told to me. That was all the teller knew about it and couldn't add a word more about how the sister reacted, about what happened later to her, on her street or in her town, about what they said to her, what she said to them, or why it was such a shock that she was a negro woman.

The story I was told did not upset me as much as what I learned from it about my town. I always knowed no negroes lived in Glasstonburg and wondered about that sometimes. I lived across the city-limit road just out of town on our farm and had tons of chores to do every day, so it was easy not to think too much about that town when I weren't there. Innocent-like, I wondered aloud the second time I heard the story, asking the lady at the counter who told it how come the people who took him home didn't stay longer to learn more about the sister and help arrange the funeral and burial. The woman was surprised by my question. She answered,

"Because she was a negro! Everyone on her street was the same color as her." I didn't get it. So what? I thought, but only looked her in the face expecting she had more to say. She stopped talking, finished her ice-cream quick, smiled, trying, I think, to act polite and, before she left, looked off to the side before continuing,

"Think about it. Think about what that meant then and since to the people in our sundown town." As she talked, her head turned slowly in my direction. She spoke the last two words while looking me straight in the eyes to make her point.

I was living in Glasstonburg over 4 years and that was the first time I heard it called a "sundown town." The name was mysterious but hinted at something I maybe suspected for a long time. Of a sudden, everything seemed clear but stayed unclear at the same time with my head whirling around with questions. I was confused and had to ask someone about those words. I thought right away about talking to Long Jon, Mrs. Wesley's son, who was in his last year of high school. I knew I could talk to him and ask him anything. And he knew.

"Everybody else in this state knows this is one of the so-called sundown towns," he explained.

"But what do that mean?," I asked, talking the way I used to, without thinking.

"Well, it's referred to as a sundown town," he went on, without showing a reaction to how I asked the question, "because negroes can come here to shop during the day, carry on any business they might have, but after sundown are not allowed in town. It's not official. It's not written, or evident in any law, of course, but a negro who comes here after dark, especially on his or her own, risks harm to life and limbs. They know to stay away. Back in the day there were lynchings here.

"So the people in this town are all white. They believe in segregation and fear negroes moving in. Many of the people on the Southside for a distance north of our house are poor and ignorant, came in old jalopies a generation or two back to escape loss of work with hopes of finding new jobs in the factories here. Some had to stay, so the story goes, when their vehicle broke down or even ran out of gas, because they couldn't afford to get it fixed or fill the tank to get further. But the politics and prejudices of those people are shared pretty much by the rest of the residents of Glasstonburg. Sundown is a term pregnant with meaning for me. What I mean is that the full ugly truth about the people who live here is revealed only after the light has left, after the sun sets, contrary to the usual idea of light revealing the truth. In this town, it's the opposite."

My first thought hearing his words was wondering where my head was all those years. How come I never paid attention to the truth about what was around me? But not knowing was in the past, and I never spent much time worrying about how things might be. I wanted to keep focused on what I just learned. Lots of times before, if Long Jon talked so much, I had a hard time understanding him, but by then I understood his way of talking and everything he said. He used words like I wanted to be able to think of when writing. Maybe, I hoped, studying, and reading the dictionary, writing so much and taking lessons with his mama, Mrs. Wesley, one day I might be as smart as Long Jon.

    Thinking about Long Jon one afternoon at work at the soda fountain, he came in with Pea-dad Cunningham. I don't think I have to explain that Pea-dad was not his real name. Long Jon and him didn't go to the same junior-high when they were younger. They only saw each other around town but never really met as friends. When they got to know each other in high school, Long Jon told me they liked each other from the start, sharing stories about similar experiences in that town. Long Jon didn't say, but I suspect that being short they both got treated the same way by many of the others. Folks in our town razzed anyone even a little different from most and made life hard for them.
    Long Jon and Pea-dad sat at the counter, and both ordered a chocolate malt. Halfway through sippin on his, Long Jon said he had to share with me a secret that only his own family and Pea-dad knew about. Then he gave me a wonderful compliment. He said that he, his mama Mrs. Wesley, and sister Pam, all felt I should know before others because they thought of me as a member of their family. I felt the same way and was deeply touched, but by the serious look in his eyes I figured that being a family member was both good and bad. I believed he must have something like bad news to share.
    "I graduate in a month. In early June when I turn

eighteen, we're leaving town to go back to New York. I've been accepted by NYU to begin in the Big Apple in Fall. New York City is often called the Big Apple. The school has promised me some money, and if we stay with my mom's parents not far north of Manhattan in Penmont, New York, I'll be close enough to commute. My sister will be starting as a freshman in high school where lots of kids will be new to one another. It won't be like she'll be the only newcomer."

    He looked for a moment in my eyes and tears started to come out of them. Of a sudden, I felt alone. The people who knew me best, who understood me better than anyone, were leaving. The town I was living in instantly seemed stranger than ever and I was scared. Long Jon seemed like he read my mind because then he said,

    "You know, you've outgrown this town too, and I hope one day you'll leave it like we're doing. All things come to an end. You should never doubt that knowing you has been great, making me feel better than you'll ever realize, but one day soon you should move on too. By on, I mean up. This sundown town can only keep you down. You deserve to continue going up".

    Long Jon weren't my boyfriend but I loved him for saying that.

    Cliff is my boyfriend. I <u>have not written</u> about him for a while. (I wrote lines under those words because that is the present perfect tense, and I am proud to show that I'm learning how to use that and the past perfect tense). Cliff lives around the corner from the Wesley family's house, only a couple of houses down the next street. I've been to his place and have heard his papa play his dobro guitar lots of times, enough to be very impressed.

"I'm the real thing, a hillbilly from heaven," his papa often says about himself. Cliff says he wants to be like his dad. Cliff plays the guitar too but wants to be his dad's partner by playing drums to make his papa's advertisement 'Drum and Dobro' more than a joke.

"It's the sound the act needs to be first rate," he claims. Cliff is hot shot playing drums, but I guess something about what he wants for himself in the future makes me feel not so good. I'll have to think about it more. Recently I've been seeing Cliff less often.

A few weeks before Long Jon turned 18, I got my 19th birthday. The Wesleys were moving back to New York, and their house was all inside-out and cattywampus with their unfinished packing. Mrs. Wesley acted particularly kindly towards me. She knew my strong desire to continue learning. I had some grammar books she had loaned me. She said I could keep another one if I wanted to continue to study. I told her I did. "Examples with Corrections of English Grammar Mistakes" was the title, and she said it was the most practical and easiest to use grammar book she had ever come across. She gave me two other books to keep about using Latin to expand knowledge of English: "Learn Latin to improve your English" and "How Latin Teaches you to Think."

Learning Latin was a new idea to me. We had never talked about other languages, but Mrs. Wesley said I was ready to push forward and discover how the

English language had been formed. English was half German and half Latin, she said, mostly from French. She used the expression "Latin cognates" and said the more I could learn about them and how they influenced English, the richer my feeling for our language would be. The magic words she used were that studying Latin would help me learn "to think straight and be guaranteed to make me smarter."

Mrs. Wesley repeated more than once that they all thought of me as part of their family. She left sentences unfinished while talking about moving, like as if she wanted me to declare I wished I could join them. I never did and she never went so far to suggest it herself. Maybe she wanted to and maybe I wanted to, but both of us held back. I remembered Long Jon's words about all things coming to an end. Thinking back, I believe I was a little excited by the idea of improving my skills with the new books, because that is what I did, but at that moment I forgot Mrs. Wesley and Long Jon would no longer be nearby.

Our goodbyes were full of tears. Saying farewell to that family seemed unreal, realizing then that I would be on my own with the books without Mrs. Wesley as a guide. She said she had faith in me because I had already proven my "determination."

She, Long Jon, and Pam got in their car, drove down the driveway to the road, turned right and, as they all waved goodbye, rolled away into the distance. I felt like I was drunk, still not believing it was happening. We promised to see each other again, but the only real thing my head could hook onto was that I had some taters to peel for dinner that night.

That evening after we ate the taters from the field that I <u>had mashed</u> (past perfect), beans from the freezer that I originally picked from the garden and pork steak from one of the slaughtered hogs with mama's Jell-O desert, I was laying stretched on my bed down in our bedroom. Knuckle and Brain were cleaning up in the kitchen. I don't know why I was thinking this way, but I started wondering why I never saw Jer or Moon Boy clean up in the kitchen or set the table before we sat down to eat. They just came when called after ringing the dinner bell or just showed up, chewed along with the rest of us, then cleared out to do whatever they wanted. Jer was about the same age as Long Jon and, like him, just finished high school. He wouldn't be around much longer since he was going off to college in another state before end of summer, so he was beyond asking to help with house duties, mama said.

But Moon Boy, too, had never raised a hand to do chores in the kitchen. I knew he and Jer worked sometimes running around helping their dad, but still, I figured if things were right in this world, being as how he was part of the family, he should have jobs to do in the house. It weren't the first time the thought had crossed my mind, but while feeling sorry for myself being abandoned, I felt what it was like to be at ease in my body stretched out across that comfortable bed without more housework to do, so I started to wonder how come only us girls had household jobs, as if we were born to it.

To escape getting bogged down in my notions, I opened the first book on the small stack Mrs. Wesley left me that was in my reach laid out on the bedspread: "Learn Latin to improve your English". It started out almost the same way as the Spanish language book I never learned much from back in high school, except 'amo', 'amas', 'ama' and so forth, in Spanish, was 'amo', 'amas', 'amat...', in Latin. I knew Spanish had come from Latin, but it didn't dawn on me until then that knowing even a bit of Spanish meant I must already know some Latin. I turned more pages. It looked like a regular primer to teach the Latin language, except every chapter had sections with part of a page, an entire page, or even several pages, shaded a different color that showed English and Latin side by side with explanations. I wondered if that was what Mrs. Wesley meant by "cognates?"

 I didn't do anything anymore without my dictionary, so I looked up the word 'cognate' and found a string of explanations, but the only one that had a meaning I could understand was, 'allied or similar in nature or quality', followed by an example that helped even more.

 'For example', it continued, 'the Latin word, 'pater', is father in English'. I jumped on that because 'papa' is even more like 'pater', it seemed to me. These two words, it finished by saying, are cognates because they are similar. With that last statement it was settled.

 I understood and stopped thinking about everything else, even for the time being about my stepbrothers. Before Knuckle and Brain made me turn out the lights, I had run through lots of pages in that book looking for Latin-English cognates. I found out the word 'cognate' itself came from the Latin root 'cogn', meaning in English 'to learn'. Examples of English words that come from that root, such as 'recognize' and 'recognition', are words I knew already, but other ones like 'cognition' and related 'cogitate', are ones I didn't. I wanted to learn those groups of related words in English, along with useful Latin expressions and how Latin came to leave so much of a trace in English. So, I learned something about history too – old history that took me back a few thousand years.

Sometime before she left, Mrs. Wesley made sure I wrote away so I could start studying for GED exams. In May I turned 19, the age when it weren't necessary to get permission to apply to take the GED. It was a countrywide program and states awarded the certificate, to those who passed the tests, as equivalent to a high school diploma. She said that with my "stick-to-it willpower," I was certainly able. I didn't have to explain how come I had no diploma. I only had to follow the rules, so the grader was certain I had studied the material and it was really me who took the tests. The folks running the program were strict about that, and there were special places where I had to set up appointments to take the different parts of the test.

I think in some ways those tests and preparations were harder than if I'd stayed in high school with the other kids. While still nineteen, I passed all of them, doing best on the English language part that was split up between vocabulary, grammar and so on. I wrote to Mrs. Wesley and told her the happy news. She answered that she was "really proud" of my achievement and knew I could do it. I was all Ya-Hoo! and grins, but secretly wished I'd done better with mathematics which was the hardest for me. I had to take that part twice and passed it the second time hanging by a thread. And I knew that the state officials who prepared the tests watered down (an expression I learned from Long Jon) the math part to what they thought all kids should know coming out of high school. I knew from Jer that he studied harder math, first year Calculus, which I know is way beyond even algebra, which was still almost a mystery to me.

While studying for those exams, I met other people preparing to take the GED – all kinds of people, and not so young ones either. Some were immigrants with interesting life survival tales to share. One man, who was almost 30 already, after being with a group that smuggled themselves into our country in a ship, somehow got a job washing dishes in a restaurant. He wanted first off to learn to speak English. He taught himself with a book he stole and by talking to as many people who'd listen and talk with him. His story sounded much more challenging than mine because I had lots of help in my learning. He told me he lived under the street one winter in a vault next to a space that ventilated warm air from the subway in New York City.

My contacts with those different kinds of folks made me realize I weren't like hardly any of my old acquaintances in this town. Realizing that, I no longer felt so lonely. I thought of myself as a secret member of a group of folks looking to choose their own way. I told mama about those people, and said after years of not liking it, I felt proud of my nickname Nig. She knew why the kids in school used to call me that and asked me why I was proud of it. After thinking about it a few minutes I told her it was because I didn't like the way most of the town's citizens talked about people who were different. Knowing I was not one of them made me feel better about myself, and their nickname for me made me feel I was different. I didn't want to think like those people and liked the idea of being unique. What mama answered surprised me, because she said,

"Nig is not a name to be proud of. You already know you are not like your old high school chums, so you don't have to take that name to heart to prove it to yourself. That name is only meant to hurt you."

She said I should reject that name and anyone who called me that unless I "knew one hundred per cent that they meant it ironically."

I thought I knew the meaning of her last word because I already used the word 'irony' but looked it up anyway and learned it was the adverb form of that noun. Irony, the dictionary said, meant the use of a word or words to convey an opposite meaning. That was when I remembered that when mama said "Bless your heart*!,*" the way she did sometimes in North Carolina, she was being ironic because she really meant the opposite. Before that, I just thought ironic was another word for funny.

Now I must write about something more personal. Maybe I have a problem with boys. They are usually friendly to me. Some even say I'm cute, but I don't know if what I see in boys once I get to know them is right. Cliff, who was still my boyfriend until a few days ago, is good-looking and almost always treats me nice. I can't complain about that....but..., I started to think critical thoughts about him. I never said anything, but after I turned nineteen, he started to act almost like I was helpless or something. He started holding doors open for me, bragging about how fast he could split wood, showing his biceps for me to feel how hard they are. Taking advantage of the heat this summer, he went around without a shirt on when with me, like as if I didn't know already he has a nice torso. The way he acted confused me. He's close to 20 but seemed like he'd taken a step backwards in age. A few months ago he gave me a ring he bought for me,

"Because you are my girl," he said.

Whenever I talked to him about what I was studying, he didn't seem interested. He thought my preparation for the GED was "a good thing" but wondered out loud why "all of a sudden" I wanted to learn Latin. When I told him that knowing Latin was giving me new knowledge about my own language, he said I could speak English good enough for him, that he'd had enough of books in school and vowed he would never read another one in his life. Maybe that was when I started to think that him wanting to be his dad's partner was sad somehow.

The house he lived in was not much more than a shack, but I only had that thought about his house after he made it clear to me that he didn't care to learn anything more. Playing the drums was what he wanted to do. Once I'd heard him say too often that he didn't want to learn more, I knew he didn't care a hoot and a holler about my studying and learning. A few weeks ago, we had an argument and he said I was "puttin on airs."

Soon after, we made up enough for him to propose marriage. He told me again how much he loved me. I thought it over for the few days he said he'd wait for an answer, but I finally turned him down. He acted almost like my first boyfriend, Tad, had done by telling me I wasn't worth it anyway and that we were through. I was much sadder than when I'd broken up with Tad, but I got over it sooner than I thought.

Working at Pauli's soda fountain, I enjoy all the people coming in more than ever. I like company and I think all those folks help me keep my chin up (if that's the right way to say it). Young men, some I remembered from high school, come in, usually with a date or in a group of other guys. It is interesting to see how some have changed over the years since I left school four years ago. By now I am almost twenty. A few of them asked me about Cliff.

That's how word got out that Cliff and I weren't going together anymore. Some of those guys soon started to flirt with me I think, at least they seem to like to kid me about little things more than before to make me laugh or to act sugar-nice like Cliff did when he first came up to me in the shop. I like that and enjoy myself, but I don't want to be pulled into anything with any of them and always give some excuse. I weren't always sure how to react, so just try to stay neutral, I think you'd say. I admit, though, that it is good for my self-confidence, and, without lying about it, flattering. I knew it couldn't last.

Maybe I was too neutral. Or maybe I showed that I didn't think the same way as those young men and women about a lot of things, even as I was learning to talk more correct like them. Since I didn't fall for any of the guys or anyone's line, it was as if they were thinking I put myself above them, so they had to pull me down. It may be, too, that what started out as feeling different made me act, without knowing it, like I was better than the others in town. Maybe those young bucks picked up on that attitude and didn't like it. I wasn't playing their game.

One young man I recognized as someone who'd been in school the same time as me, called me "Nig". I told him I preferred to be called by my own name. He answered, "Once a nig, always a nig". A few people seated in the nearby booths laughed.

After that, it seemed like things were never the same for me there. The young men stopped flirting and never paid me much notice at all except to make their orders. No one was ever as rude to me as that guy was, but I felt like a stranger, not only in that town but also in that shop, where, it was true, before I had felt like the queen bee, but only because folks acted friendly and kind and, being on the other side of the counter, I could give them what they wanted, so they had to be nice. Then I realized that my feelings come from the way they treat me, and now they make me feel like I don't belong.

The main reason I came to feel different was because the other students I'd met when studying for my GED made me realize the world is complex and varied and has so many kinds of people in it that it's exciting. I couldn't understand why folks in my town don't feel excited by that but seem to want us all to be the same.

Before summer started, I turned twenty. It was about the worst time in my life because I just stopped talking out loud, even though my inside voice was yakking a mile a minute – mostly about the resentment (a word I got from mama) I felt with no one interested in talking to me in the shop. And it weren't in my imagination either. People just made their orders, then parked themselves in the booths. Hardly anyone sat at the counter anymore except when the crowd was so big they had no choice. Hardly anyone even said 'boo' to me. Because no one chatted with me like before, I turned inside and didn't talk to them. That was new, and I knew I couldn't last long being that way, so I started to wonder what I could do next in life to move up, as Long Jon once put it.

One day a lady who'd known me and mama almost since we were brand new to the town came into Pauli's ice cream parlor when it was empty, and I was alone behind the counter. I once heard her and mama talking back then when she asked mama if I had "always been slow." Mama answered, "Appearances can change," but that lady always acted and talked to me like I was a little girl. After making sure I knew who she was when she came into the shop, she asked me if I knew the governor's name. I told her I did, which seemed to surprise her a little. She then asked if I knew he had to run for reelection, and I told her I did.

"So", she said, "do you know he is bringing back the old 'whistle-stop' idea to campaign for reelection?" I had to admit I didn't, and she seemed pleased to tell me that he was coming through our town in two days to give a speech off the caboose platform at the back of his private train, just like politicians did in the old days.

"But he'll only speechify for a short time before the train continues on," she concluded. "You should be there so you can see how beautifully the train is fitted out."

The train, she continued, was very fancy with a private club car for him to eat and entertain guests with a separate bedroom all gussied up with armchairs and frills and the outside had lots of brass parts all polished bright and shiny. I replied,

"Sic transit gloria mundi," and her mouth fell open like as if I'd hit her with a stick. After what felt like many seconds with her looking at me with her gaping mouth as if she'd never seen me before, she blurted out,

"What did you say?" I repeated the words and told her they were Latin. "It means, 'So passes the glory of the world'," which I quoted from the book I'd been reading that said it was a "commentary on the vanity of worldly glory." She stammered that she didn't know I knew Latin.

"You are Abigail Boone, aren't you?"

"The same", I answered, and she said,

" Well, I swear. You certainly seem different. I can't believe you're the same girl!" She rushed out, shaking her head as if she'd run into a person she thought she knew but who was so unlike her memory that they might as well have been a stranger.

That woman helped me in a way. She showed me how much I really had changed. She taught me I was unusual and ...unexpected. I started to think up thoughts.

I knew I wanted to continue my studies and hoped to pass on what I was doing for myself to others who didn't yet know their worth. I decided to apply to the teachers' college in Yankton City, twelve miles away, and wrote to them right off. I got accepted for the fall of 1960 based on my GED results.

There were two tracks in the training, one for elementary and one for high school. I wanted to work with elementary school kids and didn't have a choice anyway since I had no specialty to offer to teach high school. I felt excited to be moving up like Long Jon would have said. The school year was to start in a few months, and I didn't ask further questions that might have given me answers that would have startled me.

***

During that first college year, after turning 21 in May, I continued to live at home on the farm. Nothing was the same there anymore, neither my family, nor me. I left early each morning to go downtown to catch a bus to Yankton City. I commuted both ways at different times to get to work in the ice-cream parlor, depending on my class schedule. The morning bus ride, though, was a time when I could prepare for the day.

Jer was away at college. Knuckle and Brain had some of my chores to do plus their own. They were then thirteen and not interested in anything but boys and themselves. Moon Boy was a senior in the Catholic high school, involved in lacrosse, wrestling and the farm where he worked off-school hours for his dad. He put in a little time with his schoolbooks, but truth be told, not much. We did not talk a lot, nor did he ever take part in dinner preparation or later clean-up either, which I noticed, of course, but I didn't care much anymore since I was planning on moving out.

I shared with mama my plan to move to Yankton City. She agreed it was a good idea, but we hardly had any time to talk serious-like. Maybe in her mind she figured my fixing to leave was only natural and expected. She had the twins to worry about and The Menace was turning out to be a handful that distracted her to no end with worry. She'd always felt protective towards him. The result was she no longer had much time for me.

Thanks to commuting, I was able to continue working a varied schedule serving sodas and ice-cream. Folks were coming into the ice-cream parlor more often those days to gossip about our new president from the democrat party who nobody liked or trusted. But their coming in was good for business. Sugar from the ice cream seemed to fuel folks' negative thoughts and comments about our "youngster democrat president from Massachusetts," some called him. He registered so far to the left for most that they felt the need to do something to organize against him.

People seemed to like gathering more and more in Pauli's parlor as 1961 progressed. It seemed to me that sugar had even become a replacement for alcohol. I wondered why those people didn't go into the bars to vent their anger at what the new president was doing to support negro people and their petitions, which practically none of the towns' folks favored, until somebody told me that drinking in a bar in this town was like admitting failure and defeat. Most didn't want to be seen in them.

They wanted to plot and gossip among themselves for ideas to make sure that man was not reelected for a second term. The best place to hold quick meetings was to sit in our booths where four people could talk quietly without bother from others, free from the chance that one of the group, heaven forbid maybe even more, would drink too much, and turn the meeting into a farce.

The year went that way through summer, and I continued to play my part. I kept my white skirt and red and white-striped top outfit clean, stiff, and starched, and the boss was happy to see the till full at the end of each day.

"It's good for my bottom line," he often said. I kept mum, not joining in the conversations in the booths, staying quiet since I was just the hired help, expected to wait on the customers. My ideas were pretty much set in my head against what I heard, so I felt if I voiced an opinion I'd soon wind up without a job. I needed all the money I could get since I was saving up to move away.

Before the end of that first year of teacher training, I learned by word of mouth from other students, and from private talks with a few administrators, that for future teachers who had chosen the elementary path, there were two-, three- and four-year training options to choose from depending on where in the country and in what school one wanted to teach. I didn't understand those various options at first, but when I finally did, I was surprised in a very unpleasant way. It was not spelled out in the school's manual. I soon figured out that the options were not written anywhere because they would have violated federal law that came after the decision in the supreme court case Brown vs the Board of Education.

I had been so naïve. I thought overturning the separate but equal idea I had read about, starting back in 1954, the year I arrived in Glasstonburg from North Carolina, was being respected as the law of the land everywhere by 1961. I found out that, No Abigail (I scolded myself), if I wanted to teach in many southern states, or some school districts in the north, I could choose the two-year option because the standards for teaching in schools for negroes in those areas was lower than for teachers who wanted to teach white kids. And segregation in many school districts was still the rule.

I had never given any thought to it before, but the more I did, the more I felt it was the negro kids I most wanted to work with. Being allowed to teach those kids based on a lower standard, however, wasn't what I had in mind. To the contrary, I thought it was appalling. I found out, too, that I was one of those singled out (new expression for me) by the school administration to be given that option. Nobody ever explained at the time that because of the records they had of my school background, I was considered a likely candidate for the proposal.

As soon as I was pulled aside and told all this in private, I started to ask around about schools in the area. I learned that right in that town was a K–8th grade school, built with money from the Clarendon Foundation that targeted colored kids in the segregated negro community. The school was in a very good quality building with up-to-date supplies and books, an unusual investment for that foundation in this northern city because most Clarendon schools were built in southern states specifically aimed to give negro kids the same advantages for learning, at least with completely modern supplies and in new buildings, that many white kids had. At minimum, teaching in the Clarendon elementary school required a three-year teacher's training certificate. It was too early to apply, but it became my goal to try to teach there when the time came.

Chapter 3

I continued to work at the ice cream parlor the summer after my first year at the teacher's college. In late August, I left home and the farm for Yankton City, and got a little apartment within a fifteen-minute walk from the college – twenty minutes if I weren't in a hurry. Hoping I had put aside enough money from my years of working, for the first time since childhood I felt what it was like to be able to give full attention to my studies. My specific goal had been to continue improving my grammar, to remain focused on learning Latin, and getting good grades to impress teachers. I wanted to show serious accomplishments for when the time came to find a teaching job.

The language arts class didn't offer much in the way of challenges, but I was surprised when I felt riveted (new word) to my seat when the professor for the mathematics training gave us examples of techniques to use to teach elementary school arithmetic. I came to feel I had learned enough about English grammar by that time and was looking to replace that passion with a new goal I had set for myself for ways to teach arithmetic concepts to elementary school kids.

***

The name of my next-door neighbor on the third floor of the apartment building was Agnes Short. Our apartments were just under the roof. She was maybe five or six years older than me. My flat was clean, though minimal in size. I rented with the idea of keeping my costs low.

In time I realized that certain items like the range, the fridge, the water taps, etc., though still functional, were run-down and not always reliable, but I stayed until Christmas of my third year of teacher's college, long after my 22nd birthday had passed. Agnes never invited me into her apartment, never told me what she did for work, how she paid her bills, her groceries or made her rent. But I never asked either, since I figured it was none of my business and she was always distracted or busy when I saw her. We did not become friends, only exchanged friendly words when we sometimes met in the hall.

A well-dressed colored man, whose name I learned later was Reginald Steffens, visited Agnes from time to time. When he saw me the first time, he did a double-take and asked Agnes, who was clinging to his arm as they were stepping out of her apartment, "Who's she?", as if I weren't there and he couldn't ask me directly. Agnes told him quickly I was her new neighbor, Abigail, and gave a little tug to lead him toward the stairs. Reginald resisted long enough to turn and say directly to me this time,

"Whatever your color, you're not negro, so you can choose whatever part of town you want to live in. I'm down for that if it means I get to know somethin about the folks livin here. In your case, I approve." Agnes kept her arm locked in his as they sauntered (new word) down the hall to the stairs. Reginald did not look back, but something told me I would see him again.

It was late in September. After several nights he knocked on my door. When I opened, he held out a flower bouquet. He was all politeness, telling me he wanted to apologize for being rude to me when we first met.

"I should-of said something like pleased to meet you and welcome to Midtown Apartments, instead of what I said which wasn't polite to say to someone I don't know. I own this building and when I can I like to know who's livin here."

I was surprised to see him at my door, then by the flowers followed by his words. But when he said he owned the building, I accepted the flowers and invited him in, though suspicious why he'd come to my door without Agnes, who I assumed was his girlfriend, though it was obvious he was more than ten years older than her. I felt hesitant in the situation. Thankfully he did not step inside, explaining that if there were things in the apartment that needed fixing, he would give me numbers to call to complain or arrange for repairs. Then he gave me a look of confidence, declaring,

"Agnes does jobs for me and I want you to know we are only friends." Then he winked at me, tipped his hat, and said goodbye.

I was perplexed and a little confused, but Reginald made his intentions known soon enough. The next time he came to see Agnes, he asked in at my door to find out how things were going. Again, I thought it would be rude not to invite him in. This time he did not decline. I made tea and laid out cups and saucers with some banana bread I'd made. Meanwhile he got comfortable on the sofa. Right off he told me that only occasionally did someone not of his race live in his building. He said,

"I have ways to know who lives here but I don't normally get involved with my renters. In your case, I feel fortunate to have met you beforehand and compelled to make an exception."

I asked him directly about his relationship with Agnes. He surprised me when he got up, left, and returned with Agnes from across the hall.

"He's not my boyfriend, if that's what you're thinkin," she said. Reginald then added,

"Call me Reg, as if sayin edge with an R in front. It's shorter, and I like it better, especially when a pretty woman like you uses that name because it sounds friendly and more intimate". After giving her tea a few sips, Agnes gave an excuse to leave and, before leaving, said,

"See you later baby."

I was then alone with Reg, and he lost no time telling me I was different from most women who weren't negro, not only because he could see I was what he called "indigenous", but because I acted natural around him. He said he thought I was cute, and even suggested that he could show me around the city to introduce me to people he knew who were in positions to help me if I needed it. He kept saying "No strings attached."

It was so much flattery as far as I could tell. I had lost my virginity already, and knew enough about men to know what he wanted from me. So, I told him that I weren't the game he was looking for. He laughed. Hearing that from me seemed to please him, and he said I was funny. Instead of backing off and staying away from me, however, he accepted my words but did not change his ways that day or any time soon after.

Reg came to visit often. We started a pattern. I was flattered by his attention and liked him enough to play along up to a point, but always refused his advances. That seemed to spur (new use of that word) him on. He always joked with me and was persistent in making many barely camouflaged sexual offers. I always told him honestly that I wasn't interested. He never crossed the line I insisted on, however, and kept his hands off me. It was more like a game to him that he liked to play.

When he saw my two Latin language books, he acted impressed and said,

"I know some Latin too I'll have you know. I know 'quid pro quo'! And I know that means somethin like 'You scratch my back, I'll scratch yours'. That's all I'm asking from you. So, wha-da-you say, Abi? Let's do some quid pro quo! I got no interest in continuing the 'status quo'!" He laughed, thinking, I believe, that he'd gotten the better of me with his Latin rhyme.

Reg had started a new game, but I was ready.

"If we did as you want, that would be 'cui bono'? – good for whom? For you, maybe, but not for me. 'Utamerio, amabilis esto' – If you want to be loved, be lovable - and right now, rather than lovable, 'Me vexat pede'. In other words, you are being a pain in the ass!"

Reg and I both laughed. He clapped his hands in what felt like true appreciation of my Latin quips.

"OK, maybe you win," he said, but he did not yet admit defeat. Ever resourceful, he got in the last word that I had no answer to but to keep on smiling. He said,
"You know Miss Boone, I like you 'per se'."

One day, after I had told him why I was there, where I was from and what my interests were, he said I should find a good man.
"He's the man you didn't know you wanted. He's a straight arrow, no jive, colored man who lives in a town only a few miles away."
Reg then told me he could set up a meeting between us if I was interested. I was not sure how to respond. But I think in this case Reg knew me better than I knew myself, because, well, maybe I was ready again for a man in my life, so I decided to accept what he called a "blind date" with a man he named Walter Rawlins.
I saw from that offer that Reg was ready to arrange a date for me with another man even after I'd turned his own offers down multiple times. Because his gesture showed he really did intend to be helpful, I realized he could be a gentleman – at least when it came to me.

Physically, Walter Rawlins turned out to be better than I expected. He was neither too short nor too tall (5'-10" to be exact) for my own 5'-3", a difference in height I felt comfortable with. He seemed better educated than me, so I avoided talking about my background. I could see he had a nice build, no potbelly, and had facial features that made him enjoyable to look at. He was only three years older than me but seemed more than a little reserved. I wasn't sure if he liked me and I began to wonder from things he mentioned if he refused to get close to a woman not from his own tribe, so to speak.

Nevertheless, at the end of that evening, during which we saw an Elvis movie after eating in what he called a "soul-food" restaurant, he asked me for another date. I felt relieved and glad, mostly because he had not rejected me. I was interested in seeing him again. During our next date, I hoped he'd ditch his reserve and open a little so that I could get to understand what he was all about.

During our next evening together, I wanted to get to know Walter better, but the date ended with me feeling frustrated that he had not told me enough to satisfy my curiosity. On our last date, however, he finally told me more than I expected – about his background and a lot more too.

Up to that time we had always met in Yankton City. He told me again that he lived in a town called South Hope, just beyond the outskirts of Yankton City.

"I'd like to tell you more about it," he picked up from his former comments. "Between South Hope and Hope, the next town to the north, is a separate section of South Hope called Ironside Tract where my family lives. I still live there with my parents and two brothers, there being no other place in that town I could go. Let me explain.

"Only negroes live in the Tract. We are not able to live anywhere else in South Hope. On the other hand, all the kids from the Tract go to South Hope High School.

Glasstonburg, where you used to live, is well-known to all of us in Ironside Tract, believe me. It is known all around the state, in fact, but you can see that our town of South Hope seems different because negroes and whites all go to the same school.

"When I was in high school, all the negro kids at lunchtime sat on the bleachers on one side of the gym and all the white kids sat on the other. Hardly ever did the kids mix socially at noon times. Down the middle of those bleachers ran concrete steps which served as a barrier that only occasionally some of the white jocks, all boys of course, crossed to joke with one of us negroes on the same sports team, me included, to act like what they thought was how we acted, or so it seemed to me. Never was there any flirting that went on between boys and girls of the different races: no secret lovers or love affairs that I ever heard about. And, to tell the truth, you are the first woman I've ever dated who isn't my race. I was shy of you at the start and have only gradually gotten used to talking to you.

"Even with a negro girl I don't normally talk so much, but now I've started I want to tell you about the whole situation in my town. Anyone can see immediately when they cross into the Tract because they leave the paved road and pass onto gravel once they cross that invisible line. Why that is was explained to me recently by a white man who lives in South Hope. Growing up, I never really got a full explanation.

Legal documents were prepared ages ago when the two towns separated into unique jurisdictions.

Ironside Tract didn't exist yet, so it wasn't included in the agreement. Once it was created, neither of those two towns wanted the cost of paving streets there or any other expense associated with Ironside Tract, which was attached for tax purposes to South Hope. With a few legal tweaks, the agreement between them served both to ignore our community, leaving it up to my forbears to take care of their own roads. Since we have no visible government other than the tax collector and police, and given that most people in the Tract are poor, the streets stay unpaved to this day.

"That's only half of it. Our houses are on large lots. The reason for that is that we all have septic tanks and drain fields. No one is hooked up to a city sewer because South Hope never extended its sewer to serve us. ...Even though the kids go to the same school, the town turns its back on our people.

"I'll finish with the ultimate slap in our faces, and I'll admit I'm angry about this. South Hope has a community outdoor pool with grounds around it for volleyball and grass for kids to play and lie out in the sun all through the summer – white kids, that is. You see... the town fathers had it all figured out. We go to the same school, but legally we negroes from Ironside Tract are not residents of South Hope. To get into the pool, you must be a legal resident, so no negro kids to this day, thanks to strict segregation and legal trickery, are ever seen on the grass, in the pool, or anywhere inside the cyclone fence around it.

"You lived in a sundown town that we all know about. You've seen those basketball games, I suppose, and witnessed the way the Glasstonburg crowd behaves, right? Well, except for the fact that South Hope isn't a sundown town, the result isn't that different."

Once again, I felt so naïve. There was no way I could have known those details, but I guess I had been blind to a lot of things. I felt honored that Walter had not only opened up but had shared all that with me. When we parted that night, I felt he wanted to kiss me, but he hesitated long enough so maybe he lost his nerve. I was sorry he did.

The next time we met, Walter came by to see me after letting me know he was coming over for a few minutes only. It wasn't a date, but he had something he wanted to talk to me about. He asked me if I had time to take a walk. Our walk turned out to be much more than that.

Having something important on his mind, Walter began by saying,

"I've been meaning to ask you for the last week, Abi, but couldn't figure out how to put it. We, my family that is, are having a reunion at our place and…uh… I wonder, … if I ask really nice,… if you'd like to join me to meet my parents." Walking by Walter's side, after a moment I stopped, wishing he hadn't felt the need to add "ask really nice," and, looking at him real bold, trying to seem like it was natural for me, said,

"Carpe Diem, Mr. Rawlins." Surprised, he asked me to repeat and asked,

"And what do you mean by that?"

"It's Latin", I answered, "meaning 'Seize...

"Yes, I know," he interrupted quickly. "I've heard it before and know what it means. I'm just surprised to hear those words, especially from you and especially in the context. If I'm not mistaken, it sounds like you mean to encourage me." I kept my head turned towards him but lowered my eyes. I didn't feel quite so bold as I continued.

"In other words, I mean...you should do and say whatever you feel is...right. ...If it's what you really want...you should make it yours." He looked even more intently at me.

"You're a real surprise, Miss Boone!" He laughed and popped the full proposal on his mind:

"If it doesn't disrupt other plans you might have, I would be honored to chaperone you to my family's reunion next Saturday at our house."

"How can I refuse when you ask in such a fine way? Of course, I'd be very pleased." Walter and I walked on. He looked neither forward nor backward, but kept looking at me by his side, and, without asking, took my hand which pleased me even more. To tell the truth, I couldn't take my eyes off him.

***

Before the Saturday of his family's reunion, I received a letter from the teachers' college where I was taking classes. The drift of it was that despite my good grade in the English language portion of the GED, several of my professors in the program had noticed while talking to me that I seemed to have some deficiency in English that I needed to eliminate, especially in my uses of the past tenses of 'to be'.

The letter went on to say that I should continue classes, that I was not being asked to leave and that I was sure to become a wonderful teacher. It was only that the school did not desire to advance individuals who did not show top level proficiency in English.

I was flabbergasted, wondering what the author of the letter, the dean of my department no less, was referring to. I couldn't imagine how I had missed something so basic. After wondering how to answer the letter, I got the idea to call Mrs. Wesley. Of all people, as my mentor for several years, she knew all my abuses of standard English and might help explain the letter to me. She certainly did. After telling her about it near the end of our talk, what she told me in response was a revelation.

Right away on the phone, she and I got caught up on our news. I told her my mama, Jasmine, was in good health, gave her an update about the Jones kids, such as I was aware, that I currently lived close to Glasstonburg in Yankton City, had recently begun my second year of teacher's training college, and loved it – some of which she knew already. It was Mrs. Wesley's turn because I did not choose to discuss amorous issues with her that were unknown as to how they might work out. On the other hand, I was very curious to know how things were for her along those lines.

"I have met several men, but none so far seem right," she disclosed. "I'm still interested, but it's such a chore! One man who I thought I liked at first, on our second date started saying shocking things against Jews. You know I'm not Jewish, or even very religious, but I cannot abide that kind of prejudicial talk which often indicates serious personality problems. So, the simple answer is, I am still looking when I have time."

Mrs. Wesley told me to call her Ellen now that I was an adult, and she was single. She reminded me she had worked many years as a professional research librarian before coming to Glasstonburg and still had the job I knew about at the library in Penmont. She said Jonathan (I still thought of him as Long Jon) was a junior at NYU and getting excellent grades.

"He has so many interests that he is trying to get the NYU administration to allow him to design his own major."

Her daughter Pamela, she said, was happy in the local high school and had made a few good friends, doing her best to cover up that Pam was not quite the student Long Jon was. She quickly changed the subject.

Living with her parents was working out well because they were happy to have her and the kids in their home,

"to help them stay young and at the same time give them support as they grow old. My father is now 73 and has developed a few motor issues. It's just that I'd rather not go into it over the phone except to say that he tells me all the time how lucky he feels that we're here. I'll give you the details in my next letter."

Taking the pause as my cue, I read her my school's letter. She knew exactly what it was all about. For the first time since I'd known her, she apologized.

"As you know, we librarians have the tools to research many things, which has always been almost an obsession for me. When I was tutoring you, I took an interest in North Carolinian expressions and grammatical quirks. I knew that having spent your formative years immersed in that culture, you used certain words in, how can I say? ...Non-standard colorful ways... some of which I hoped you would not lose. They carried such vivid imagery and sounded so unique. I admit I never thought your writing would get beyond...home, you see. To put it succinctly, I did not correct everything you said because I wanted your language to retain some of its original flavor. To make my point clear, in both writing and speaking, you used the negative plural past tense of 'to be', 'weren't', without regard to the number of the subject.

"'Weren't' is reserved for plural subjects. In other words, in both your writing and speech you used — and apparently still use, at least while speaking — 'weren't' as if 'wasn't' didn't exist.

"Now, I must apologize. Obviously, I am not perfect. My enthusiasm at that time is coming around to haunt us both. Because I never corrected your oral usage of that word it appears I have gotten you in trouble. It's certainly no fault of yours. You had no idea your usage was an embedded oral habit that was not standard English, and I suppose I really didn't foresee it would become an issue. This is new knowledge to you which you will have to 'sapere aude'."

The Latin expression Mrs. Wesley had used meant 'dare to know', which she knew I had made my motto soon after my first letter to her to tell her how much I was learning from the books she gave me. I had to write down only one word while we spoke over the phone to look up later.

In her next letter, she explained everything, adding that uses of the verb 'to be' were less clear-cut than she had told me on the phone. 'Were', and 'weren't', can be used properly with all subjects, singular and plural, when used in a subordinate clause which is "subjunctive", she said, a clause that introduces doubt, most commonly after the word 'if'. She listed a host of examples, explaining the rarity of the subjunctive in our language, but insisted that to be considered literate, I should use the subjunctive forms when speaking standard English.

I was lucky that because I write so much, I was able to find some specific examples of my wrong usages. I even found examples in the grammar book she gave me. So, in truth, it was not all Mrs. Wesley's fault. I used the grammar text she had given me often but had somehow missed that important detail. There were plenty of times when I could have thought about what I was writing or saying to verify their correctness, though I must admit, 'wasn't' still sounds strange. I know it'll take me a long time, maybe years, to feel comfortable saying, for example, 'I wasn't excited to go to the party' and not 'I weren't excited to go to the party'.

We agreed to stay in touch on the English grammar issue and I resolved to think longer and harder before allowing my mouth to carry on the way it always has. Maybe that is why people have started to take what I say more seriously.

***

I met Walter's family that beautiful Saturday in late October. Feeling a little self-conscious, trying to hide my uses of non-standard English that I had just become aware of, I wanted to be discrete and not talk much. Walter's mother assumed I felt shy around negro people and that I didn't know how to act naturally around them. Some of the things she said to me sounded odd at first and, as the day went on, struck me as almost aggressive. She asked where I lived and was surprised that I lived in the negro neighborhood in Yankton City.

"What do you want to live there for, girl? You may be brown, but you've still got lots more choices than we have." The thought struck me that she might have assumed that being non-negro, the world was my oyster, as some say. Trying to be friendly later, I told her that Reginald Steffens had become a friend and had set up my first date with her son. She didn't let that pass without comment.

"Reginald's a scoundrel and a skirt chaser. He especially likes non-Negro women, so it doesn't surprise me he's after you. You've got to ask yourself why he'd set you onto Walter? He might be usin you for somethin." I tried to tell her that we had what felt to me like a true friendship, and I replied,

"After he realized he couldn't score with me, I think he decided to be a gentleman, and he proved himself to be a true friend when he arranged for me to meet your son." Walter's mother gave me an odd look, shook her head, and went off to talk to someone else. She just turned her back on me, cutting me off. I was trying to like her but for some reason she didn't like me.

Walter's papa and brothers were friendlier towards me. His younger brother told me Walter had been a talented basketball player. Even though he was not particularly tall, Walter played on the first-string high-school varsity team. I asked Walter about his basketball career since I had known people who played that game in high school.

"One", I said, "we called Possum," and before I could go on with more information, he surprised me by beginning to describe him.

"How do you know what he looked like? Don't tell me you had to compete in Glasstonburg!"

He pulled me aside, where others couldn't hear him, to describe some of his experiences in my former town, having played for his basketball team there "too often," he informed me. I could tell that revealing his feelings about it was not easy for him, that he was trying to control anger and hurt which he did not want the others to see or hear. He told me that before playing in

Glasstonburg, and in one other town, the coach had to prepare the players.

"We were only boys, fifteen, sixteen, seventeen years old, and easily intimidated," he explained. "The coach told the players to try to always stay completely calm and read us a poem called 'My Motto' by a negro poet and playwright."

Walter said he had repeated the following couplet so often to himself that he felt it was his own motto. He recited it, saying it was only part of the poem:

"I play it cool and dig all jive,

That's the reason I stay alive."

The coach, he said, almost preached to the boys to ignore what the people in that town might say.

"He told us that we were on our way to play in hell and that the names, maybe things, hurled at us would not hurt us if we didn't allow them to 'touch' us. To 'stay alive', as the couplet seemed to say, depended on staying cool."

I wanted to tell Walter about the times I had seen out-of-town teams with negroes playing against our team in Glasstonburg but knew this was not the time to tell. He was still alive, as the poem said, but he had been hurt and was housing anger that went back to when he had first been called the 'N' word and understood it meant he was hated for what he was. I began to agree with what mama had said to me once not to be proud of my nickname Nig. I saw how right she was. Walter and all other negroes had to live being called the full version of that name by the majority, and it could only have spawned (new word) deep resentment in them, I figured. The time to share my experiences could wait. How long that took did not matter, since by that time I was beginning to feel attached to Walter.

So far, Walter's mother has never warmed up to me. I got the impression that day, reinforced since, that she suspected I was Reginald's girl, sent to spy on the family. I couldn't understand why she might assume that, unless there was some bad history between Reg and her family to make that man seek revenge.

Since then, she seems to have dropped that notion, but then started asking me questions that suggested I was "slumming" (her word) because I am not negro. I took that idea, if she meant it, as a terrible insult to her own son, who I looked up to for his many fine qualities. Now I wonder if she is against me only because I am not of her race. I had heard of black people who are racist. If that <u>were</u> (I'm proud to show I've learned to use the subjunctive) the case, I decided her feelings might be justified, having earned them the hard way. I decided not to judge her but not to let her opinions "touch" me either.

Remembering my step-brother Moon Boy's paper napkin joke that carried on with the theme 'There's only two things to worry about, either you're sick or well', I knew this family had lots of things to worry about – most obviously, but only for starters, needing money to put food on the table, to keep cars running, to repair things on the house, to pay medical bills, and on and on.

Behind all that was the way white people had stacked the deck against them and all others of their race. I decided only adolescent kids, or drunks, found such paper napkin jokes funny or believable because adolescents had not yet learned the ways of the world. But even adolescents worried about lots of things, so I figured the paper napkin had been well placed for drinkers trying to escape their worries at the bar where Moon Boy found it.

Thinking about that joke, I got a flash in my brain in the form of the clear memory of mama telling me she was part Cherokee but didn't know which part. Just like when the sky clears and gets blue as the sun appears, shedding light, I understood during that moment that mama had made an ironic joke when she said that. She wasn't serious!

That made me wonder about the paper napkin joke, thinking it may not have been literal but ironic too. I think I had always heard what was said to me in a literal way before that. From that moment on, things people said to me began to make more sense. Knowing about the existence of irony added valleys and hills to an otherwise flat space in my feelings about the world.

***

At the end of that school year, I continued to commute in the other direction to return to Glasstonburg for work during summer at the ice-cream parlor. We decided it best for Walter not to visit me in Glasstonburg, particularly during the day at my work, so he never saw where I was employed. Each year the crowd in the shop increased, so the owner was glad to have me back during the busiest season.

Mama visited me often in Yankton City where she met Walter several times. She developed a warm feeling for him, but I did not know how Mr. Jones, or his kids, would react if they knew I was involved with a colored man, so I kept my personal life to myself when visiting the farm, preferring to keep it that way even after the summer was over.

Beginning my third year in school I had more worries than I relished. I had been unable to save enough money to live for more than a few months in the apartment, even living close to the bone, as we used to say in North Carolina. I would be obliged to find another job during that last year of college. In early November I got lucky. How that happened was a godsend since I was almost at the end of my savings. I had never had strings pulled for me before.

It was that same angel Mrs. Wesley who came to my aid. The last year she had lived in Glasstonburg, after she and her husband separated, she sought part-time work in Yankton City as a librarian and wound up working there full-time before the family moved away. Since we frequently corresponded, she knew I needed work. I'll eliminate the details. She set up an interview for me at the central library in Yankton City, where she was well known and remembered. Based on her positive and enthusiastic recommendations, I was included part-time as a paid member of the staff, returning books to shelves, checking them out to borrowers, orienting users and taking partial charge of the reference section.

Shortly thereafter began a whirlwind period of my life when so much happened I still can't believe it. Two days before Christmas, almost at the beginning of 1963, Walter and I got married and we moved into a larger apartment in the same building. Both my mama and Reg came to celebrate with us, but to be honest, I was so happy I hardly remember them being there. I had married the wonderful man I admired and loved so much! I know, I shouldn't express so much happiness or be so self-centered to express it, but I can't help it.

I got pregnant almost immediately after our marriage, and had not a care in the world during the following months except to continue with my schoolwork and check on the health and progress of the fetus inside me. Near the end of that school year, I began to show obvious signs of being in the family way. Then I graduated. It seemed anticlimactic (a word Walter once explained), what with marriage and pregnancy and a newborn on the horizon. I decided to forego looking for a teaching job for the next school year after the expected birth in September to dedicate my time and attention to nothing but my baby.

My baby boy came in September 1963. I had carried him all through that hot summer and was glad to have Walter heft him about for a time. The baby was a beautiful and chubby little thing, so content and smiling as he seemed to gaze at the world around him. Almost from his first day, we called him our Little Buddha. My own contentment and happiness could not have been greater, and Walter was proud to carry little Buddha against his chest when we went out.

Reginald, who had become quite a good friend of mine and Walter's, came to the party Walter made in the apartment to welcome home the new mama and her baby from the hospital. Reg had changed his behavior towards me and seemed to enjoy seeing Walter and I together, almost as if he wished he were Walter (subjunctive again).

An exchange occurred at my homecoming party, started by Reg, that could easily have ruined the celebration, had it not been avoided by Walter's intervention (a word that seemed very useful when I learned it).

Walter had invited one of his friends to my homecoming. His name was Waldo Smith, and he was so big we all looked like midgets next to him. I could almost have predicted his nickname.

"The brothers call me Tiny", he said after Walter introduced him.

Reginald replied, "Call me Reg", using the same words he had used with me, but then added,

"My last name is pronounced Steffens, not 'Stevens' like some people seem to want to call me." I think Waldo meant no harm when he remarked,

"Why care, it's a slave name anyway?" Reginald stiffened as if hit by a lightning bolt, and, straight as a ramrod, lifted his head as high in the air as he could manage, and aggressively said back,

"Well, negro, I see there's lots of things you don't know!" His answer took my attention away from ogling my baby. I didn't want a possible argument to disturb my bliss, so I glanced a look at Walter for him to intervene and smooth things over. Walter excused his friend, who looked just as surprised as the rest of us by Reginald's reaction, and asked Reginald to share the story of his last name.

Walter succeeded in shifting the attention away from the outburst, and Reginald seemed to relax a bit as he related,

"My great-great grandfather was made a free man by his owner. The family moved up north and took the name 'Steffens', to honor my great-great grandpa's brother, Steffen, who had died of tuberculosis not long before. My name's not African, but because we chose it, it ain't a slave name neither. My honor to educate you, big little man!"

Waldo, or Tiny if you preferred, had the good grace and sense to apologize, seeing that Reginald was still miffed (I like that word too), and thanked him for the explanation.

After that, Waldo and Reginald behaved themselves and everything took place amicably. Mama was there too, of course. She did not get as flustered by the interchange between the two men as I did, maybe because in her family growing up in North Carolina they often had lively arguments. Even so, she was not shy to make her offer to help look after the baby loudly known to all of us. I refused her help.

"'Not 'til I get a full-time teaching job," I answered, knowing secretly that I'd likely need her help sooner than that.

Mama was beside herself, showing joy in her new grandson, and looked happier than I ever remembered her being. As she held the baby she called him "my flesh and blood", and fussed over him more than she had with The Menace. Holding her grandson in her arms, she looked like she had rediscovered the world.

By the time of that homecoming, we still had not found a name yet for our baby and knew there remained only a few days more to choose one. We laughed about wanting to christen him Buddha because of the perpetual benevolent look of contentment that he seemed to cast on the world around him. We knew, though, that giving him that name would be putting a label on him that everyone would misunderstand. It had to stay between us. I wanted to name the boy Walter II, after his papa, but Walter ruled that out, saying,

"My son should not be known as a knock-off of his dad but as his own man, known for himself alone, as a person who stands on his own two feet for what he believes."

I understood his feeling about that. Our agreement ruled out that one name among hundreds, but it didn't help us get much closer to naming our baby. Mama suggested a few Cherokee names for boys that had attractive meanings, but they were too long, too complicated, or too hard to say.

We looked in some books and soon had a shortlist of names we both liked. Their appeal was partly for how they sounded with Rawlins and partly for the meaning the book gave each: Oscar – God's spear; Nolan – noble or renowned; Peter – stone or rock, Roscoe – heartland of the roe deer; Andres – manly, brave or warrior, and Khalan – strong warrior. Walter pitched at first in favor of Khalan because of what it meant. He also liked its sound next to Rawlins. I liked Roscoe for the meaning, which could connect him to his native heritage as well as the alliteration (a word I learned years ago from Mrs. Wesley) with Rawlins. But we ruled that one out too. In truth it had little relevance in meaning to what we were looking for.

I dared not say it since my husband was a soldier, but was relieved, not to say surprised, when he said on second thought that he was uncomfortable naming his son a fighter, warrior, or soldier, like him. That did not fit his hope for his son to be his own man.

What Walter was really searching for in a name was that his son would hold firm to his beliefs. That one decision ruled out for good Khalan, Andres and even Oscar – all of which had an aggressive meaning. That left only two: Nolan (noble, renowned) and Peter (stone or rock). Together we chose Peter because it most closely fit the meaning we were after. Also, most people knew what it meant, which was not the case for Nolan.

Walter had joined the army a few years before, assigned to recruit in the negro community in Yankton City and to enlist potential soldiers he believed good prospects to become what he called "advisors" in the U.S. military to be sent to an area of the world where our government was getting more involved. The country's name was Vietnam. I had to search for it on the map to learn its location. As 1963 progressed into the Fall, American advisors were being sent to Vietnam to help put down insurrections and other troubles that were building up there. However, they were not supposed to get involved in combat. Close to the end of that year, the president of Vietnam was assassinated, and events began to pull our government more closely into what was happening there in a military way.

Despite hoping to be exclusively with my baby for the entire first year since his birth, in the new year 1964 I went back to work part-time at the Yankton City library in the reference section.

Walter seemed to be of several minds (an expression I learned recently) about the overseas events in Viet Nam. He often spoke of the U.S. presence in Vietnam lightly, comparing our country to the rabbit in the Uncle Remus "Tale of Brer Rabbit", punching the immovable tar baby who refused to get out of the way on the road, first with one fist, then the other, followed finally with both feet, all of which became stuck in the tar until thoroughly sucked in and immobile. Walter laughingly joked that the U.S. being pulled into the politics and struggle in Vietnam was not unlike that rabbit who unwittingly got pulled into the tar baby that would not obey him. On those occasions, Walter seemed carefree and light-hearted, seemingly not affected by the unfolding events.

Nonetheless, I could tell Walter was troubled, not with doubts about his role or the events in Vietnam, my first suspicion, but with his own bottled anger. As always, he confided in me. His words came across like a memorized speech that he'd been trying to articulate to himself for some time:

"I struggle with the same monster all the time: my anger. I want to be seen and known as equal to others, free to be myself, judged on the same footing as all other men. I've chosen to enter the very system that is always ready to misjudge and keep me down unless I prove myself 100% beyond reproach. If I reveal my anger about being treated in a prejudicial way, I'm lost. Holding that back is becoming harder for me as I get older. The coaching I got as a teenager playing basketball is wearing thin."

Before the end of September 1964, shortly after Peter's first birthday, Walter was under a lot of pressure to volunteer to go to Vietnam, which he did. He rationalized in favor of doing that, believing he had learned to control his anger and convinced himself, and me, that if he could demonstrate his competence as the lieutenant of a small, mixed white and negro platoon of advisors, functioning as mentors to the Vietnamese army, he might eventually be promoted to captain, just as he had already made lieutenant. He saw a future for himself in the military.

    The Army enlisted him within days for that duty and lost no time detailing him (Walter's word) overseas, first for further training in Japan before sending him to Vietnam. He was soon on a plane, leaving Peter and me. I wept. I begged him to stay. I argued vainly that he had nothing to demonstrate, or prove, to me.

Chapter 4

That spring I mailed my application to the Clarendon school for a teaching job in the fall. Though I had hoped to be invited for an interview, when the invitation arrived, I was very excited. My confidence was with me the day of the interview because during my three years of training, professors had encouraged and often praised me. I think I explained well my motivations to teach. I was overjoyed to learn afterwards that I was shortlisted for a second interview!

My happiness faded as the day approached for the second one, beginning to feel nervous and negative about myself. I had no idea what I could say that would make them want to hire me instead of someone else. The administration members of the Clarendon School jury that conducted the interview, told me that my motives to teach were quite good, but several of the interviewers wanted me to explain why as a non-negro I wanted to work with negro children. They asked me so often, trying to pry more out of me, that I decided to tell them my entire story: my childhood and youth in North Carolina, moving up north, living on the farm, my nickname at school, being made to leave school at 16, my writing and slow learning that improved with constant work under the tutorship of Mrs. Wesley, preparations for and earning the GED, working in the ice-cream parlor, witnessing the racist attitudes of many folks in Glasstonburg, wanting to leave, my desire to teach younger kids to help them realize their potential, my move to Yankton City and enrollment in the teachers' college, my marriage with a negro man and now being mama to a beautiful baby boy. I told them that I suffer knowing that negro children, my son one of them, will have to struggle to escape all the racial tags given to them by the white majority, and that escape can only come through more awareness to be gained through education. I am grateful that the period when married women weren't allowed to teach is gone, because back then I wouldn't have been able to follow my calling.

I finished by expressing the hope that they realized from my story how important education had been for me personally.

When I left that room after having talked so much and for so long, the panel of three people was quiet. Nobody said anything other than "Thank you Mrs. Rawlins." My thought was that they would not want to allow a retard like me to work in their school, but once I decided to talk about my life, it all just tumbled out. Two days later a letter came from the local Clarendon school's administration. In so many words, it said the following:

> You have been unanimously selected to teach the 5th grade class. Our heartfelt congratulations

to you. Your personal story far exceeds what we hoped to discover in applicants' motivations and was an inspiration to us all. We feel fortunate to welcome you among us.

That really put me in a Yahoo! mood. I was so happy I danced around the apartment with Peter in my arms without turning the radio on for music. I didn't know my story could have inspired anyone, not even sure that was a good thing. Now I'd have to live up to their expectations. I sat down, wrote a letter straight off and addressed it to Walter. I was going to be a teacher! Then I remembered Mrs. Wesley and wrote her a letter too. Except for giving birth to Peter and marrying Walter, I was experiencing the happiest moment in my life.

I began to take action to get prepared to teach. Studying the fifth-grade curriculum especially inspired my keenness to tackle the program for mathematics. My tentative plan was to reinforce English with references to Latin through the back door, so to speak, blending it with arithmetic and numbers. After all, story problems in math use English, I rationalized, which are full of Latin cognates. In truth, however, I had no idea how to approach doing what I wanted to achieve. My excitement would show me the way, I hoped, starting by going to the school building.

A month before classes began, I bought a special paint that had to be rubbed with paint thinner to be removed, so the erasers we used couldn't take it off. I brushed one hundred lines four inches high and about one-and-a-quarter inches apart, having calculated beforehand they would fit. When done, they looked like a row of sticks standing vertically – or soldiers standing at attention. Then, with the same paint, I added a continuous line across the bottom which could represent, in one's imagination, the ground that supported the sticks – or the soldiers. I called the lines "the rector" and located it near the top of the board so that it wouldn't get in the way of using the main area below. As a final touch, using the same paint, I wrote '0', '10', '20'... up to '100' under each vertical line where the count landed. Though finished, I wasn't sure where my effort would lead.

***

It took some time to get used to standing in front of a bunch of kids I wanted to inspire who did not appear at first inclined to be inspired. For a few days I wound up using some of mama's way of talking. Making threats, I learned which kids responded to that and which didn't, like the difference between Moon Boy and his brother Jer. I finally decided just to be myself and talk to the class naturally. I wasn't sure what that meant, but it had to do with being relaxed and staying as honest as I could, responding thoughtfully to what each child said – and giving each one credit for talking.

After several days with kids asking about the lines painted on the blackboard and with me only answering in a vague way because I was not ready to use the rector, believing the kids were not ready either, more and more kids asked questions about it. I realized that not bringing it up myself had been a lucky stroke. Their interested curiosity, which I did not put there, came from them alone. That was the best part. I told them I called the lines 'the rector', writing the name on the board, which was in a language called Latin.

"It is a Latin word and means 'ruler', like a king". I continued with the following question, trying to be non-committal,

"Why do you think I call it that?" One boy named Willie said I should know because I named it. Still getting to know these kids, I felt that boy was resisting being pulled into my game. He seemed older and probably had more to offer in the long run. After acknowledging his remark, I decided to persevere with the question despite his making fun of me to see if he would be influenced by the other kids who seemed more enthusiastic. That, I was glad to learn, was how it turned out.

"It's like the ruler my mom had to buy for me to bring to school, but mine only goes ta twelve. Yours goes ta one hundred," one girl said.

"Thanks much for that", I said, "because it will start us off. We can use your suggestion to continue. Can you think of other meanings of the word 'ruler'? Here's my word", and I wrote my suggestion, 'di<u>rector</u>', on the blackboard, defining it and pointing out that the English word came from the same Latin word as 'rector'. With their eventual suggestions, we had my word, 'director', "ruler like a king" and "someone who tells you where to go, like a guide."

I thought the reference to a guide was a wonderful insight from that same boy who essentially told me I could answer my own question. A girl brought up "the golden rule" and the kids talked about that, explaining to each other what each thought it meant.

I threw out the question,

"Do you think these words are connected somehow in meaning?" The kids did not understand me. I realized I had to express the question differently and use different words to be understood – another insight I gained that day.

"I mean, how do you think these words are alike?" A boy who hadn't spoken so far, volunteered without raising his hand,

"They're all helpers, like tellin us rules."

"You mean, like in games, basketball for example, rules that everyone has to obey to be able to play together?" The boy smiled and nodded. He was pleased that I understood, and chose that way to show it, without words.

We hadn't even used 'the rector' the way I intended yet. Nevertheless, I had had my first real talk with the kids and a little trust was growing between us. I resolved that my style of teaching had to be with the kids choosing the way. I would be their rector, or "guide", the wonderful word that boy had used to define my role.

The rector became my guide – eventually. Our discussion did not end there that day, thanks to my students. Their curiosity as to why I put those lines on the board did not fade. I didn't know if they were ready to push further into the mathematical concept of percentage that, according to the curriculum, they were introduced to the year before, but it was supposed to come after a lot of practice with fractions.

On another day, I pointed out that Helena, the girl who said her ruler only went to twelve, had mentioned the big numbers, but in between those big numbers were smaller lines creating equal spaces between the big numbers. Without my asking, several kids started to count on their own rulers, and I heard the number "sixteen lines" called out.

"We learned about the ruler in primary school!", some shouted critically at me, as if I had brought up baby stuff. I had to think fast to "guide" them back onto the discovery track.

"OK, I know that, but we are all getting on board a train that will take us to bigger ideas than your rulers."

"How many lines does my rector on the board have?" I asked. "One hundred!", most of the class shouted back.

"One hundred, we will all learn, is a helpful number to make it easier for you to learn more about fractions and percentages. Unless you already know, fractions and percentages are really the same thing, but written, and used, differently. Yes, the rector on the board has 100 lines, but can anyone guess why? What's special about 100?"

It turned out nobody knew or wanted to guess. I started to give hints.

"My drawing shows one hundred lines, but what it represents (I felt compelled to explain that word) is called a 'meter'. Does that help? Any ideas – or guesses even?"

Everyone just stared at me. Obviously, they knew nothing about the metric system.

"In our country most people use inches to measure things: we agree that there are twelve inches to a 'foot', we call it. And we call it a foot because an average size grown-up's foot measures about 12 inches – or one foot. Each foot, as you just said, is twelve inches. Each inch is broken down into smaller parts, sixteen to an inch. Can someone remind us how to say the measurement I will now draw on the board?"

To represent a ruler, I quicky drew a zero, a number one and a number two spaced evenly on the blackboard in a row, and between the 1 and the 2, sixteen lines as evenly as I could manage. Each line represented on 16th of an inch.

Halfway between the one and the two (the half-inch mark) I started a circle that surrounded the ruler from zero to that 8/16 th point.

"How do you say that length?" I asked. Some kids already had their rulers pulled out and one boy was the first to raise his hand. He said,

"One and a half." He had beaten the others and I praised him for being first. Then I asked,

"Is there another way to say that measurement? I'll give you a hint: can you say the measurement using the name of those small lines in between the one and two?"

The kids were confused by my question. Part of my purpose was to get a sense of how many of them were familiar with the measurements on the ruler, but my question was too wordy. Words were getting in the way of the concept. However, one boy, who was obviously ahead of most of the others, said,

"One and eight-sixteenths of an inch."

"Bravo", I replied, and meant it, but a glance around the room showed me confusion or non-understanding from many of the others. In that way, I realized, without having to give them a test, that these kids were shaky when it came to fractions.

Next day, I began to refresh their memories. It was early in the second week of school after summer break and they needed to be refreshed, so I decided to start right away. The curriculum called it doing 'equivalent fractions.'

I did my best to elicit answers from as many kids as possible to the point that I felt most were comfortable saying 2/16 was equivalent to one eighth, that 4/16 meant the same as one quarter, that 8/16 was another way to say one-half, and so on. My idea was to build enough confidence in my disciples to delve a little deeper into fractions as an eventual introduction to percentages, which was why I originally drew the rector.

I concluded by emphasizing that most countries in the world, including American scientists, use what is called the <u>metr</u>ic system to measure things. That system, I told them, is based on the <u>meter</u>, a word from another ancient language called Greek that came into English from Latin. It meant, simply, to measure. A meter, I informed them, is one hundred <u>cent</u>imeters, smaller than inches, that break the meter into one hundred parts, just like the 'rector'.

I had to go easy with a lot of them. My intention was for all to understand.

"Raise your hand if you know," I asked next day, "that the rulers you bring to school are all exactly the same length." Everyone raised their hands.

"Why is that necessary?" I pretended to wonder aloud. What followed was total engagement from them, explaining to their uninformed teacher the reasons why we must all be on the same page. I agreed, reminding them that Roger had said in class, "They're all helpers, like tellin us rules." He remembered and, on that day, by quoting him so exactly, our bond was strengthened.

Without rules, I cheerily agreed with my students, such as having our classroom rulers all different lengths, would be like living in chaos. That led to searching for a definition of the word chaos.

The kids' ideas for definitions ranged from "no rules," to the cryptic remark, "nothin' is funny or sad anymore". Talking after class to the girl who had given that last definition, she volunteered somewhat different words to explain.

"I was thinkin", she said, "about there bein no fun and no games, that everybody would be so different they couldn't have fun together, ever agree or even talk together so nothin would be funny or sad and no fun." I thanked her for staying to explain. I told her that her definition was very smart and even very wise.

She was more imaginative in her definition of 'chaos' than the dictionary, I told the class next day. Nevertheless, I read how the dictionary defined it, followed by the story of the word's origin.

I wanted every day to include some information about the origins of our language in our discussions about mathematics and other subjects.

Eventually, we did get back to the rector. Several students reminded me that we had hardly touched on why it was there. Some tried to erase it, only to find they couldn't, so figured it must be important.

The time had come to put the rector to use. Starting at what my students would consider a "baby" level, I brought some rolls of pennies to class and explained that all of them had fifty pennies in them.

"Here are two rolls, each with 50 pennies. With the two rolls together, how many pennies are there? Already, almost all the kids were shouting out "100!"

"Thank you for playing along with that," I said, "so here's my next question." (Fractions had been introduced the year before, for some maybe in third grade, but I never wanted to assume and particularly never wanted knowingly to insult or demean anyone with remarks like "I know you know this already", if, in fact, they did not).

"What fraction of 100 is just one roll – or let me ask that in another way. What fraction of 100 is 50?" I was gratified that almost all their hands went up (they had been well trained about proper behavior in the classroom, I could see). But someone shouted without being called on: "One-Half!"

"Right. Now, I'm going to tell something, but then you must use what I say to answer the next question. First, when you have one hundred pennies, you have a dollar, because our money system is based on a hundred too, just like the money systems in other countries. Now, my question. Can anyone tell us another name we often use for the word 'penny'? Several hands went up and a girl said, "a bad penny".

"What is 'a bad penny'?" It wasn't the answer I had hoped for, but it offered me an opportunity to learn about something I didn't know.

"I never heard of that before." Our roles were reversed. I became a student, and the girl was my guide. The other students saw and understood that I was sincerely interested. I think that helped grow more trust between us.

"A bad penny is what my dad called my older brother when he came home after bein gone so long."

"That is very original", I said enthusiastically. "Tell me more." Willie, the boy who had spoken out several times in our mathematics discussions, volunteered these words:

"My mother once told me that a bad penny is a person who did wrong. A bad penny person is dirty and got no value until clean. That's what my mother said anyways."

"So", I said, "if there are ten bad pennies, with no value, in my roll of fifty pennies, how many good pennies do I have?" I wasn't sure where I was going with this.

"Can I ask that question by using another word instead of penny? In other words, I'd like you to use another word for penny in your answer."

"Everybody knows that", offered a different girl I hadn't heard from yet. "You got forty good pennies, or forty cents."

"Very good. Thank you! Another word for penny in English is <u>cent</u>! That word comes from <u>cent</u>um which is Latin and means 'one hundred' or 'one hundredth'. It can mean both, depending on how it's used. I wrote 1/100 th on the board, but suggested they could also call it just "one over one hundred", if they wanted.

A penny, or a cent, is one hundredth of a dollar, the money we use." I was careful to talk slowly, using equal signs, such as penny = <u>cent</u> = 100 to the dollar, on the board.

"In Spanish, a language that about as many people in the world speak as English, the word <u>cent</u>avo means one hundredth (<u>1/100</u>) of their peso, the money they use. In France, <u>cent</u>ime is the word for one hundredth of a franc, the money they use. And the French word for one hundred, when they count, is also <u>cent</u> = 100. All those words come from the Latin word <u>cent</u>um.

"What does all this have to do with the rector?", I queried, looking at the board. Already, the rector had an identity for us all – a shadowy ghost up on the board.

"For once, I'm going to try to answer my own question. There are one hundred <u>cent</u>imeters in a meter..." I wrote '1 meter' = 100 '<u>cent</u>imeters' on the board, "...which is used to measure in most countries outside the United States - not to count.

"The rector is not a real meter because meters all have the same length, just like our rulers, and the rector is much longer than a real meter. The only way it is the same as a real meter is that it has one hundred equal parts.

"One hundred is a valuable number to help guide us to learn more about factions and percentages," I went on, repeating what I had often said before. I then showed my students a real meter stick which I had obtained with the help of the school. Comparing it to a yard stick (three feet I reminded them), they agreed it was a little longer.

"When you-all are a bit more comfortable with fractions you will learn that per<u>cent</u>age (I wrote the word on the board in that way) is all about being a part of, or more than a part of, one hundred, which is the same idea as a faction. It is just another way to say the same thing as a fraction. <u>Percent</u> is a Latin word. In Latin, and in English, it means 'per hundred' or 'for each hundred'. For example, one half as a fraction is ½, but it is also <u>50/100</u>, fifty out of one hundred, because fifty is one half of one hundred. One half, ½, is also 50 percent or 50%," which I wrote on the board like that.

I did not expect my students to grasp firmly any of those truths from my words. They needed practice and lots of it. At long last we started using the rector. For their first lesson, I circled the rector lines up to ten, then followed by circling twenty lines, followed by thirty lines, and so on up to 100. They had to write in their notebooks each percentage, after I taught them to write the % symbol, explaining again that 10 % simply means 10 out of 100, or 10/100 (ten one hundredths) or 1/10 (one tenth), and so on. From that point I showed them that any number of lines, be it 10 of the 100 lines, or 64 of the 100 lines, or 150 lines (50 more than the rector showed) could be expressed as percentages: 10%, 64%, and 150% respectively.

Then came the equivalency experiences that took most of them several months to internalize. Once they got the idea, it all became obvious to most. I was on the lookout for those who did not get it and gave these students special tutoring. I believe I succeeded with almost all of them, if not all. In that way I had to remain dedicated, assuring myself that everyone eventually understood the idea.

"Going from fractions to percentages is just a matter of words", I said repeatedly.

This led to reviewing numerator and denominator – both important to help convert fractions to percentages. Teaching (or reminding some of them) about that took a lot more time. To change 3/8 to percentage required several steps by dividing the numerator (3) by the denominator (8) to get .375 which meant 37.5 out of 100, or 37.5 %. Combining all these operations meant they needed also to know how to do long division and how to manipulate the decimal point.

The rector helped them progress and stay enthusiastic. In my excited ignorance I had placed the rector up high on the board, so most kids had to get on a chair to use it. When standing on a chair, the student could be taller and play teacher. That student could then circle parts of the rector and ask questions, which they liked to do, acting out the guide role.

I was particularly happy when I saw students converting percentages back to fractions. I will paraphrase a group of students in an exchange I witnessed that occurred right before the end of the year:

"Now that you said 55%", the guide, Debra, pronounced standing erect on the chair, "who can name the fraction for that? Randy said fifty-five over 100, fifty-five one hundredths (which the student guide wrote on the board as 55/100). Now who can reduce that further? Sandra said divide both the numerator and denominator by 5. OK. So Randy, what does that give? Yes, I think that's right, 11 over 20, or eleven twentieths (11/20) the guide wrote on the board). And as Miss Abi told us, we know you can't make 11 any smaller."

Besides teaching about decimal points, I had to teach some notion of prime numbers to my kids for them to know when a fraction could no longer be reduced.

I was very lucky to have had such an enthusiastic group of students and it was a successful and personally gratifying first year. Unfortunately, the student mix was different each year, and I had to wait several years before another group was close in enthusiasm and responsiveness to my class that first year.

***

The school year ended and Walter returned during summer from what he told me was an early "reprieve" from his one-year "tour of duty". I realized immediately that his presence filled a void in me, left dormant, that I recognized was yawning wide. I felt hunger for his body. Even our fingers touching, intertwining in slow motion, was sweet magic. After his long absence, like the Earth after a long drought, I was ready to be irrigated and nurtured. Languishing across the bed, feeling his familiar warmth, I felt almost fulfilled by what I had not known for too long. I would have reached the stars, but for something that was missing.

Walter was passionate and seemed as happy and relaxed as I, but I felt something different in him, as if he were not entirely there or was not sharing everything with me. I wasn't sure and didn't understand. He seemed to have trouble confiding in me, which had never been the case before. One evening during his second week back, Walter finally got over his recalcitrance (new word), or whatever it was, and simply told me that he wanted to re-enlist. I acted unsure of what he meant only because I did not want to believe what I suspected.

"Re-enlist? I know you don't mean you want to rejoin the army since you're already a professional, so I guess you mean you want to go back?" My voice became shriller as I spoke, almost sobbing as I got to the end. He only nodded. Finally, "Yes" came from his bowed head.

"You understand, sweetest love, that as a soldier I must make a choice. You know I am not obliged to go back to Nam, but if I don't, I can kiss my ambitions goodbye."

"What ambitions?" I pleaded to know.

"I got within a finger's length of making captain. Promises from my colonel are that for sure I'll make that promotion when I go back. The army is really ramping up our presence in Nam. General Westmoreland has been approved by President Johnson to supply another 200,000 troops. They're all green. It's the perfect situation for me to be in since I have proved myself as a trainer and leader. The army needs me enough to give me higher status."

"You're needed here too, loved and needed and...". I couldn't finish because Walter was trying to convince me, telling me about what he'd experienced over there. He talked for the next ten minutes trying to fill my void with his enthusiasm to return, not only for promotion but for a host of reasons that, in truth, I lost track of as my grief increased. Finally, I just begged him to stop.

"Please, please Walter, you don't have to continue. I guess I'm convinced, but please stop talking about it."

I had him with me for only a little over two more weeks when his R and R ran out and he had to return to do his duty. I loved him. I needed him. I wanted him and did not want him to leave. It was as simple as that, but not simple because at the same time I understood his sense of duty, of honor, and, most importantly, the assurance he gave me that he was on the right track to "prove" himself, which he said more than once. I could almost feel his torment which had such a long history behind it.

The day of his departure we hugged and kissed for a long time, my tears flowing non-stop. The longer our parting lasted, the more I didn't want it to end. Eventually, Walter had to lift my stiff arms from around his neck. As he held my hands in the air, to the side, then against his chest while kissing them, he gazed into my eyes assuring me of his love and that he would soon be back. Neither of us brought up his intentions about what he wanted to do after the end of the next "tour of duty."

We exchanged letters even more than we had done the year before, maybe because that previous year my mind had been so engrossed with proving myself to the school, the other teachers and to my students. I received a glowing letter from Walter dated around mid-November, in which he sent me a copy of his promotion to captain. I was so happy for him that I felt his advancement almost vindicated his decision to go back. I just yearned even more for him to be with me. He also briefly discussed the numbers of recruits who were arriving in droves off airplanes daily from army camps in the U.S. They all needed further training and orientation and he assured me that he would not be involved in combat while training them. This turned out not to be true.

In mid-December a letter was delivered to me personally by two uniformed army officers. In the letter the US government wrote that Walter had received a medal posthumously with great honor. He had been killed on a reconnoitering mission with a group of soldiers he was training and died a hero. It awarded me his captain's pension. The piece of paper the letter was written on fell from my hands. Its contents felt like a mockery to me, a complete travesty because the army had taken my husband from me. From that point on, I hated war and all it stood for.

I started to cry, even as the two uniformed men were at my door, and began to wail as soon as they left. It was all I could do to hold myself together to continue teaching. After a two-week leave, somehow, I managed to continue.

Before the beginning of September 1966, I had learned the trick of separating my mind into different parts. That was the only way to bury prostrating feelings that could have turned me into a depressed invalid. It was enough to help me finish my second teaching year and embark on my third. But then Fate thrust up the story of Walter in Vietnam to haunt me further. It took several years after that for me to accept that it was better to know the truth.

Several months into the 1966 school year, a letter came from Waldo Smith. In the first sentence he reminded me who he was and of the time Walter invited him to the small party in our apartment to celebrate my return from the hospital with my newborn baby.

'Reg was there', Waldo wrote. 'He and I almost got in an argument. Something crazy silly about his last name, but Walter steered Reg away, so it got defused before it went anywhere'.

I remembered the time and Waldo Smith too. He meant no harm in the things he said, I remembered having thought at the time, and he seemed unaware of the impact his words made on others, but he seemed a little one-dimensional, like someone who got attached to an idea and stuck with it, thinking it was right, no matter what anyone else might have said, thought, or felt about it.

Reginald's words that evening years ago at our party also still stuck in my mind, and I remembered that Waldo's nickname was Tiny.

Waldo asked for a get-together because he wanted to share some information with me about Walter. I froze reading his note, certainly not because I wanted to forget Walter: the opposite. I still felt very fragile and didn't want to start crying talking about him. Nevertheless, we met in a shadowy back booth of a café where I led us. It was a weekend. I arranged for Peter, recently turned three, to be looked after by his babysitter. Peter had no memory of his papa Walter, but as Peter reminded me of his father constantly. It was thanks to Peter that I hadn't gone insane with longing.

Waldo was even bigger than I remembered. He made the chair he sat on and the table in front of us look like children's toys. He started by excusing what he had to tell me, sensitive he was, he claimed, that less than a year had passed since Walter's death, but he had always believed in full disclosure. Feeling a bit hesitant, not totally reassured by his remark, I nodded anyway, agreeing that he could go on.

"You remember Walter originally recruited me," he said. "The army kept us together after that, having mysterious motives that no one can divine. I re-upped after my first R & R, like a fool. I did that cuz during our first year we Americans were still what they called "advisors" and didn't get into the fighting. I thought that would not change, but during my second tour it definitely did.

"New bloods were comin over daily off airplanes, straight from boot camp. They knew nothin about what the reality was in Nam. The Cong made it like hell, because we were fighting in jungles where we could barely see off to the sides where we were walking, and ambushes happened all the time.

"Walter and I were together when he died, so I know the circumstances. He caught a bullet trying to save one of the new recruits. For that, he was honored as a hero. I know about his private life too. I know that he loved you because he talked about you many times.

But he was a tormented man. I knew about his hates, fears, and anger because we're black brothers and we talked. 'Blacks' is the new word we use for ourselves: We're all blacks, not colored or negroes anymore. I learned to call us that from the brothers who came to Nam from out of the projects back in the States.

"Some of the top brass, though, they don't know about the language change from negroes to blacks, thinking everything will always be the same, that they'll always make the decisions and call the shots. Someone in the brass gave the order to send Walter and part of our platoon out to "reconnoiter", they called it. Me and most of the others who went with Walter that night are lucky to still be here to tell, and I intend to investigate so I can tell.

The odd thing about Walter was that he was a black captain, rare for a captain to begin with. The group of all seven of us who got sent out with him that night, were also black. Why was that? There were whites in our platoon too. And we asked why we were singled out. The answer was that blacks, "negroes" they said, would be hard to see at night and Walter was chosen to go with them because he knew them all and they trusted him.

"Where we got sent to was an area which I learned later was held by, better to say infested with, the Cong. It was a suicide mission! The brass just wanted to make sure. That's all. And Walter wanted to show himself to be a righteous leader that night, which is why he got himself foolishly killed. The brass saw us negroes, which they still call us, as expendable."

I sat in mute silence, frozen from being able to respond due to his words.

"That's the first part of what I want to tell, the easier part for you but not for me. Walter died because of outright racism, pure and simple. But...I still haven't gotten around to tellin you the rest, which I feel I have to say." I was too shocked by what I'd already heard to respond one way or the other and didn't move. I did not really want to hear whatever it was he said he had to say, but he must have interpreted my silence and rigid composure as agreement, so he kept on talking.

"In Japan, at the start of our tour, a lot of the recruits acted like men will act with the women there - the geishas, I mean. But Walter didn't participate in that... temptation... should I say? I know why – because he claimed to love you so much and thought only of you. He told me that many times. Thoughts of you were his anchor that allowed him to keep his grip on himself.

"Once in Nam, it took almost half a year for him to loosen that grip. Vietnamese women, especially in Saigon, where we spent a lot of our time, were available and willing – lots of em were working as prostitutes. But Walter still hung back. Then he met a Viet woman who was not a prostitute. She had a job that put her in contact with him and they fell into an affair. You've got to remember the stress we were under, and as our lieutenant, and later our new captain, Walter had a lot more stress than the rest of us. He needed a release".

I am surprised I didn't faint, hearing those words, but he just kept on talking.

"Anyway, that's what you should know, that he had another woman in Vietnam. To tell the truth, while it might have helped him as a man, it added to his torment, because he knew being in love with you and having her would only hurt you. I know all about hurt, but my experience tells me it's always best to know the truth. Part of the truth is that he loved you deeply. Walter was not a womanizer."

I had listened patiently up to that point. With those last words I couldn't hold back my anguished tears and raced out of the café, heading straight home. After a block, I veered off, continuing to walk. It didn't matter where to. I don't know how long or how far I walked, wrestling with Waldo's words, but finally, once back in some control of myself, I steered homeward again. When I entered our flat, the babysitter said she had just put Peter down for the evening. He had played all day, was very tired and was now asleep. So much the better, I thought.

I wrote after the occasion of my hospital homecoming when I first met Waldo that I didn't think he meant to hurt anyone – and I still don't. He was just following his simple fixation to deal me his "full disclosure", which I really did not want. He didn't seem to realize what effect his words, which pained deeply, would have on me.

It took several years to accept that Walter's actions had hurt me unintentionally and that he was wrestling with so many troubled thoughts. According to

Waldo, he loved me and suffered because of it. I eventually wondered about that the other woman, that she might also have been in love with him. It must have deeply troubled Walter that he would eventually have to hurt her too. To sleep at night, for my peace of mind, I had to forgive him.

More and more I dwelt on what Waldo said at the beginning – that the blacks in the squadron were considered "expendable". If true, it was a terrible accusation. Deniability seemed written all over it. Since I never saw a letter or heard from Waldo since, I assume nothing ever came of his investigations. His accusation will have to remain an ugly suspicion we both have to live with.

Chapter 5

Mrs. Wesley's maiden name is Ellen Ellingsworth. Over the phone she instructed me once more to call her Ellen, not Mrs. Wesley, since

"I am divorced from that man, and you are no longer a girl."

I've been getting a lot of news recently from Ellen. Things are changing in her life. Her latest epistle (from Latin epistola, which I think is a lovely word), was about her parents. Those high school sweethearts are now 83. Her papa has been in a wheelchair for several years and the couple planned to relieve Ellen from further responsibility by moving into what she called assisted living but were still looking for the right place. They asked if she was OK with them spending her inheritance in their final years. They had already made her happy by allowing her family to live in the house where she grew up.

Such issues had never crossed my mind. What impressed me most was the amount of time that had passed without me even thinking about it. When I read their ages I could hardly believe ten years had gone by since Ellen first told me about her papa's mobility issues? It was now almost the beginning of the 1973 school year.

Peter's tenth birthday is coming in a few months when he will enter the sixth grade. He advanced to the 5th grade last year, having skipped the 4th grade. His academic ability is almost scary. I know he could likely have skipped two grades and still be ahead of his class.

The time since my talk with Ellen on the phone about my incorrect uses of grammar has slipped by without me noticing the sand passing through my fingers. I wondered if I still knew any of those North Carolina expressions that she had once been so keen for me not to lose. I remember a few, but it seems memory of the rest must be buried in the back of my brain.

Several times in the past I confided to Ellen that I hoped to be free someday to follow my bent to do research. She reminded me of my secret desires which I keep ignoring.

"I wish there were a way to become a school librarian, like the feminist Ms. Young in our school", I told her once on the phone. About two years ago, I began to feel an attraction to how Ms. Young spends her days. She has access to many reference books, often giving talks to groups of kids from kindergarten through the last year of high school. For the younger kids she reads, discusses, and explains stories. She goes into much more detail with the older groups, thanks to the research she does before what she calls "sit downs". Her talks give me mountains of ideas about ways to make kids more aware of Latin, its cognates in English, history of our language and much more. But I never followed up on my desires to become a librarian, always finding fulfilling inspiration in ways to teach my classes. Somewhere in my mind, though, I crave more leisure to delve into whatever arouses my curiosity.

***

Just after that new school year began, I decided to involve my sixth-grade students in writing poetry. The academic rationale for this was to make them aware of two things: recognition of syllables (which also affect pronunciation) and creating meaningful rhyme. Rhyming, particularly rhymes internal to a line of verse rather than the ending only, seemed to come so easily to a group of three boys that I became confused. Never had I noticed such a marked difference between my kids before.

Another letter arrived from Ellen. She wrote how much she misses interacting with me and wants to see more of me. She is lonely in the house by herself, and went on to say that she thinks of me as her "eldest daughter" whom she loves as much as her real children. I was very touched by her remarks.

In the meantime, Ellen added that her parents had moved out and have new friends where they are now living. Apparently, being served two meals of tasty food each day, with waiters and waitresses, is a new treat to them. They expressed awareness that their presence had overtaxed her, particularly in the kitchen.

Her daughter Pamela had left the house and dropped out of college during her second year, explaining that after "tuning in and turning on", she chose to live in NYC. A few years of survival there pushed

Pamela to "drop out of the rat race" altogether and go out west to help start a commune.

That was partly old news to me, but I understood she was licking her lonely feelings. She couldn't help dramatizing by listing all the reasons for feeling abandoned. She rarely sees her son Jonathan (still 'Long Jon' to me) who works and lives in the Big Apple, as a recruiter for what she called a "consortium" of Ivy League schools.

I decided to phone her to cheer her up and reassure her that I love her too. She sounded very happy to hear from me, excited by a brilliant idea she had since sending her last letter.

"My question first!", I begged facetiously. "Have you ever heard the term rap?" She answered she had heard it once vaguely defined by Jonathan.

"From what he said, I gather it is a form of music, or sung poetry, words spit out quickly. Rap is catching on gradually among inner-city black kids. Jonathan is often in contact with those young people for his work. As a phenomenon, I doubt it will last."

I told her about my attempts to get my class inspired to write poetry and that a few boys had such a good feel for rhyming that I asked them if they could explain their apparent talent. They told me, in short, how they practiced making up lines of poems they chanted more than sang that had internal rhymes and gave me a few examples. They had fun doing that in groups of two or three friends, and,

"They called it rap," I said.

"Oh my!" Ellen replied, expressing surprise and admiration. "As a teacher you are either very lucky or more cutting-edge than I suspected. Rap must be spreading into the small burgs where you are, far from NYC, the be-all and end-all. Knowing nothing about the phenomenon, you stumbled onto something truly avant-garde." Once again, she used a term I was not familiar with. I humbly admitted it. She laughed, and replied,

"You have never been afraid to admit what you don't know. That is one of your best traits and has helped you get so far." She defined the expression to mean cutting edge or ahead of others.

"Now, allow me to share my idea with you. You wrote several years ago about wanting to have more time to do research and work with a variety of groups of students in schools as a librarian."

Ellen had a plan and planted it firmly. She proposed that Peter and I move to Penmont, New York and live with her as her ersatz daughter and grandson. I would pay no rent, she promised. Peter and I could convert the entire second floor for our use and she would have the main bedroom, bath and office on the ground floor. There was more to the plan. I could enroll for a master's degree in library science, and she would help me get accepted and apply for grants, if needed. She is also aware that Peter is academically gifted.

"There just happens to be a new program in foreign language immersion here, only just beginning its second year. It starts in the 6th grade for now, which is Peter's grade. Too bad he won't be with that group. But no matter. The growing program will admit new learners each year as it takes off. Peter will be able to select Spanish, French, or German, which the system is offering American kids who have no notion of those languages. For some time the schools have been offering special classes for native speakers, who are fairly numerous here, probably because Penmont attracts numbers of families of foreign diplomats who work in NYC at the consulates, embassies, or UN.

"The two best schools in town, anyway, have decided to offer these classes. They are only for the few, though, since they will seriously challenge those students who must be top caliber. They must take both the full curriculum and invest supplemental hours to learn the chosen language. I am sure Peter will be as academically challenged here as he is in your Clarendon school in Yankton City.

"Once you have a degree from a librarianship program offered by several of the universities in the city," she added, "it would be like a golden pass, enabling you to pick and choose wherever you want to work. But think of this as a plan to begin in fall 1974, after this current year."

Throughout the following months I thought about Ellen's offer. I felt adamant about wanting to stay at the Clarendon school, but at the same time I tried to convince myself of all the reasons to accept. It was the school's official reminder to all teachers, however, that tipped my decision to finally take Ellen's offer.

Just as the administration did near the end of each year, it announced that one-year, unpaid sabbaticals were available to all teachers who had worked full-time for more than seven years. I knew that possibility applied to me but had never considered it. Now, however, the school's offer was thrust on me while considering Ellen's generous idea. My stockpile of rationalizations to accept Ellen's offer came pouring in, seeming all too pertinent – and relevant. Why not take off a year? – especially if I am guaranteed my job back. Peter would flourish. The change would broaden his world. Ellen would certainly appreciate it. Reginald's words, "No strings attached", seemed true. I would be a stick-in-the-mud if I ignored the chance.

***

Now that summer 1974 is approaching, I am getting ready to leave. I often talk to mama and Mr. Jones. He seems to like Peter, though I imagine he must be a bit puzzled by him, not quite sure how he fits into his family of blonds. Peter and I do not venture beyond the farm or see the town on our visits. Mama is happy for me. She is certain I will continue to profit from knowing Ellen in ways I still cannot imagine.

"You have a guardian angel", she said one day, "and her name is Ellen, a real, living person. Few of us have the chance to know a source of benevolence, even if we are the recipients of it. You are a lucky lady."

That summer was not long enough because of all that had to be done. Just the move to Penmont, New

York was a confusing affair for me, not knowing what to take with us since I had agreed to stay until the end of the two years it takes to get the degree. if I succeed, that is. I finally decided to sell whatever we do not take with us, since I am tired of the furniture anyway and could replace it when Peter and I return. We decided to make a clean break that will allow us to imagine never returning and become what feels like wanderers across the face of the Earth – "free electrons" are the words a friend often uses.

Planning to limit what to take with me, I still wound up with five large suitcases. Peter fit all his things into two. He looked forward to the change and told all his buddies he'd be back before they knew he was gone.

***

With Ellen's help, setting up our quarters upstairs in her house did not take much time. But that was only the start. The administration personnel of Peter's future school, particularly the female vice-principal, seems quite enthusiastic about Peter. It is the oldest school in Penmont, and as such still houses elementary, junior high and high schoolers in different parts of the same building. After testing Peter during several sessions, studying his records and teachers' comments, the school's administrators enthusiastically agreed he is a good candidate for the immersion program because its rigor demands students who are highly motivated and capable. I know Peter is.

It's a real hassle getting into the graduate program, though. As Ellen advised, I applied during the former winter. The school admitted me, but not yet the department of library science that would award the degree. The administrators of that department doubted the quality of my teaching certificate that was not from a four-year college program. Almost 40% of students in the library science program drop out before receiving the degree. With such an attrition rate, the administrators repeatedly stated that with, "only a GED and a college background that reveals your other academic deficiencies", my chances of surviving the program were judged slim in their opinion.

I argued back that, to the contrary, preparing for the GED demands a high degree of self-discipline in preparation to do well without guidance from teachers. Besides, I show consistently good recommendations from the Clarendon school administrators for my nine years of teaching. I wrote up my motivations and personal story with no apologies and submitted them as part of my defense. The department's admission board has made me wait several weeks already and I still don't have their decision. I have already moved, Peter is set up and keen, so I have no intention of returning to Yankton City.

I had begun to feel depressed about being stuck in a bureaucratic merry-go-round and was getting ready to do battle when, finally, a less than welcoming acceptance to the program arrived. What it said felt like an insult. The department tacked on a full year of what they called "remediation courses" for me to complete before I could start the librarianship program.

Ellen went with me to protest that requirement, but our complaints did no good. I had to take it or leave it. We did succeed, however, in getting the school to allow close to a half-and-half mix of remediation coursework and first year research courses in librarianship. Nevertheless, I was confronted with a dilemma and a tough decision.

Initially I thought of this move as a one-year adventure into the intriguing world of formal academics. Growing more serious with my ambition to become a librarian, I had accepted that the program would require a two-year commitment. My plan had been to go back to the Clarendon school after the second year with my new degree and await my chance to become librarian. Now a third year faced me.

Even though we were free from paying rent, Peter and I had expenses. Ellen solved that by offering me a half-time job in the library where she was the head librarian. She wanted someone with former experience, which thanks to her, I already had.

Nevertheless, I began to doubt my decision to come to New York. Ellen spoke honestly and frankly to me, not about her feelings, but about the reality of the changes I would have to face later.

She said the following:

"Peter is about to enter 7th grade. I admit you had to swallow hard to accept the two-year program even before you came. At the end of these next two years, Peter will be ready for high school. Because he would have to change schools from the Clarendon establishment in Yankton City and enter high school there, you and he will be faced with the unknown by returning. There is no way around it. Do you really believe that Peter will have better options and opportunities in Yankton City?"

I had to think a long time about these facts as she presented them. Of course, Ellen's words made sense. What she was saying was that I should stay put in Penmont. We had leaped into the unknown and now had to make the best out of what we found. I decided to stay and persevere as I had always done.

When Peter's school year began, his chosen French language training consumed two hours additional each day starting at eight in the morning, rather than nine, for an hour of language instruction. Once the regular courses were finished, he had another hour of French history and culture, and was told that after the first year that hour would be taught in French. His day ended at four o'clock each afternoon, but Peter didn't seem to mind.

While doing battle with the graduate department and arranging for Peter's tests, we were visited by Ellen's son Jonathan. I was embarrassed because I kept calling him Long Jon. He fixed my problem by saying,

"From now on call me Jon. Forget about calling me Jonathan, a name you never used, and stick with only the second part of what you already know. That should make it easier." I did and it did.

Though we hadn't seen each other for fifteen years, it was curious how Jon and I got along as if no time had passed. We stood back-to-back in stocking feet and drew pencil marks on the wall. We were the same height: 5 feet, 3 inches. Settling on couches in the living room, we started with small talk, him telling me about his day-to-day life in New York City where he still got pleasure from visiting certain places that had historical meaning to him, such as Ellis Island where his grandparents had first entered the city.

After telling him briefly about Peter's academic successes, I began to tell him about my years of teaching, jokingly warning I might ask him to convert our heights to percentages of a meter. However, I pointed out that I never made my students convert between the American inch/foot system and the international metric system, only back and forth between fractions and percentages.

He held up his hand for me to wait, took out a pencil and paper from the desk, followed by his pronouncement that we were 160 centimeters tall, or 160 % of a meter. We both laughed. I told him that many of my students over the years converted the heights of the school, trees in the neighborhood and distances on the school grounds to percentages of something known.

"They loved the idea that 100 could be used for so many purposes", I enthusiastically told him.

Long Jon listened carefully with apparent interest. He asked to hear more highlights from my teaching years. I was grateful for his interest and eager to tell.

"I tried to be creative with arithmetic lessons, and some kids, usually girls, gratified me by claiming they liked those lessons best. I also tried many ways to get my students to write. It didn't matter if they were in the 3rd grade, the youngest kids I taught, or in the 7th grade, my oldest groups. For one class, I decided to use old songs to teach them how to recognize both syllables and rhymes:

"You already know how I discovered some of the boys in my class were experimenting early on with rap".

"Yes", Long Jon interjected. "Since those early days, rap has become very popular and might have a notable future. A new group called the Sugarhill Gang is becoming quite popular. Many of the youth I visit hope that group will be discovered someday and get recorded. Recording songs and getting them on the radio is what will be needed for rap to take off. But, enough about that. Tell me more about yourself."

"I haven't followed rap, but I'll give you an example of a simple challenge I put to my 4th graders to make up their own verses to tunes of known songs. Here's one verse of many from a traditional song I sang as a child:

> 'Down by the bay,
> Where tabacca plants grows,
> Returnin' home,
> My face I cannot show.
> Cuz if I does,
> my cousin'll say,

'Didja ever see a tick,
Lickin a licorice stick,
Down by the bay?'

"I replaced the non-standard words and spellings, such as 'grows', 'does' and 'didja', for standard ones, and changed some spellings to get rid of traces of dialect. I asked my students to replace the last three lines, starting at the end of the line 'Did you ever...?', with their own words. At first, I suggested they use the name of another animal and make a rhyme with the equal number of syllables as in the original.

"When starting to teach that song, it dawned on me that it was not the nonsense song I thought it was when I was a child but was about someone who left home and cannot go back because, having changed so much, he or she is either unrecognizable or unacceptable to others. In my nostalgic moments, I miss those field parties we used to have sitting around bonfires on chilly nights in late Fall back in North Carolina. In general, though, that song seems to be the story of my life. I know I can't go back to where I started life for all those reasons.

"After convincing myself that my interpretation of the song was true, I wanted students to have the same realization. I thought it would only require a little thought to understand but didn't want to push them into my adult insight. Instead, I told them to pretend I wrote the song. I invited them to ask me any question that came to mind so I could explain what I'd written.

"Not one child seemed to see it the way I just described. However, several did ask if they could change 'my cousin' to someone else. I agreed, since I had had the same thought. I told them they could use any other person, but their chosen replacement had to have three syllables, such as 'my brother', 'my father, 'my mother', 'somebody', etcetera. And since I always worked references to Latin into my lessons, all my students knew that 'etcetera' was Latin and what it meant.

"The results were varied. Some were pretty good, such as "...My father will say, Did you ever see a pig, Dancing a jiggity jig, Down by the bay." At least that one succeeded in getting the same number of syllables in the two parts. Most kids made up several verses, not just one.

"In a 7th grade class, just for the fun of comparison, I introduced the same song with an identical challenge. One student's attempt still sticks in my memory. He wrote:

'...Somebody will say,
Did you ever see a black,
Righteously talking back,
Down by the bay?'

"That boy's rhyme spoke of things beyond the poem's intent. When I read it, I instantly thought of my deceased husband, Walter, who yearned to be able to defend himself on an equal footing with his white colleagues. ...I'm getting maudlin. ...I know. There is a chance, though, that that boy grasped the poem's deeper meaning. I wish now I'd asked him."

I felt a sudden urge to continue talking because the rhyme I just cited put in my head something I yearned to say to Long Jon.

"Do you remember you once talked to me about Glasstonburg being a sundown town, and that for you sundown was the time we learn ugly truths about people? I think of it a bit differently now. I welcome sundown on sundown towns, sundown on segregation, sundown on evidence of racial hatred that goes unpunished, ...sundown on all racist thought. I mean, ...I hope the sun will finally set on thoughts, feelings and ideas that separate people. Understood that way, sundown is a thing I look forward to. I want to see sundown come to all those things but don't know how to help make it happen."

Long Jon finally spoke up.

"Sundown, as you talk about it, is what you and I are both working towards. When you return to the school in Yankton City, you will continue to plant the seeds to make that happen. You are only one person. As the saying goes, "it takes a village." Meanwhile, I am doing my bit to bring more people of color into the mainstream in a meaningful way, to "level the playing field," I like to say. White people like me must do that because we whites created the system the way it is. You can't change people's minds easily, but if we look back over time, clearly some changes for the better have been made.

"That boy may unknowingly have given you a clue to answer your question. If we understand his rhyme to mean that when the day comes when black people feel comfortable enough to talk back to power or authority without fear of reprisal, maybe that will be the beginning of sundown as you call it."

I know that I had talked a lot, as usual, and for a long time too. I wanted to learn more about Long-Jon. Turning to face him, I asked to hear about what he was doing to earn a living. He told me that because of his job, he gained access to all sorts of environments, meeting all races and types of young people, and raked through myriads of test results, taped interviews and testimonials written by college-bound teenagers. He was constantly searching for academically talented American youngsters of color, talent that ivy league schools would want to invest in with grants and scholarships, partly to distance themselves from the elitist, all-white reputations they had earned over the several hundred years they had existed, and partly because the schools he represented wanted talented students pure and simple, the best that could be found.

Jon said it was challenging. It was he who recommended the first meetings between the school authorities and what they called the talent, based not only on the statistics he unearthed but often on his personal gut feeling about his referrals, putting himself on the hook. So far, the authorities had been pleased enough with the diverse group of teenagers he sent them.

"Besides that," he said, "I think I get to know those young people a little better than the two other academic talent scouts because my height and manner make me...non-threatening...I think.

"What makes it challenging is that I must winnow the field to uncover talented youth with true academic chops while lacking full statistical evidence. I think you already must know about talent scouts who look for sports abilities. Those scouts attend competitions where they can see students' talents with their own eyes. I must make my determination of academic talent based on test results that are typically used but unreliable or misleading for the disadvantaged black and brown kids I look for. Those tests are slanted to the experiences of the majority, the white kids I mean, so I am compelled to delve much deeper, which means getting to know each of my clients, I'll call them, intimately. So far, none of the talent I am trying to find had someone as inspiring as you as a teacher."

Jon had just given me a compliment which flattered me down to my bones. I had always looked up to Long Jon, admiring his intelligence, had even hoped to be like him some day, and here he was saying admiring things to me. Then he added,

"I am going to start calling you by your full name, Abigail, not Gabi anymore, because in many ways you have changed so much you seem like an entirely different person now. I admit that if you had been on my list, then, of potential youth that I visit now, I would have been quite challenged to see you as talented, except for your persistence with my mom to improve your writing. That alone has always made you stand out in my mind as special. In fact, I often think of you as an example when getting to know those young people. Thanks to my memory of you, I look at the full spectrum of my young client's activities before deciding to send him or her to the next step."

Tears came to my eyes as Jon finished. I didn't know what to say, I was so touched. Overwhelmed would have been a better word to describe my feelings. I tried, unsuccessfully, to hide it. Choking on the words, I answered,

"You sure know how to give a compliment when you decide to give one Jon. You could have said those wonderful things a long time ago."

"I could have. You're right. I should have. I can say many things to give excuses, but the important thing is that I'm telling you now. That counts for something, doesn't it?"

Jon leaned in, then sat closer to me on the sofa and put his arm around me as tears trickled down my cheeks. I was experiencing the happiness that comes from release, a relief that came as my reward for the many years of self-control I had practiced on myself to push to learn, push to inspire my young charges and rush to love and cherish my husband and child. The release came from suddenly feeling I was recognized as a worthy human being.

Jon helped me dry my tears and we changed the subject. He told me he had gotten what he called an interdisciplinary studies bachelor's degree (self-designed studies in several areas) from NYU, then a master's degree in Comparative Literature (English, French, and German) from Columbia University and finally a doctorate in Public Policy and Government from Princeton University. I always knew he was smart, especially after he said he'd received either partial or complete scholarships to earn those degrees. Now that he was 33, he had been working at the same job for over five years.

"My job forces me to be inventive and flexible", he said, "not really creative, like you obviously must be conducting your classes every day, but I have to …innovate constantly."

Over the following weeks that summer I wondered about Long Jon, not quite sure how I felt about the potential closeness that happened between us. We had been good friends in the past and I admired him. If he wanted to become more than that now, I needed more time to think about it. But except for that once, he hasn't shown any further signs of interest. Rather than dwelling on those thoughts, I concentrated on what I do best: plunge into books to learn more.

At the end of that first year of library studies I did not foresee flunking or dropping out. I wrote a short and simple letter to the Clarendon school to inform them of my successful year and to explain why the program would take two more years to complete. As Ellen predicted, I was determined to go through with it. In my letter I acknowledged that a three-year absence was too long a time to make future promises, but that someday I hoped to return to the Clarendon school as librarian.

***

In June 1977, I was awarded the degree: not the best among the students, by any means, but certainly not the worst in grades, evaluations and "kudos received for solid achievement", to use Ellen's words.

My success does not represent brilliance on my part, only old-fashioned dogged hard work and stick-to-itiveness. Now that I have my degree, I have been hired full-time at the Penmont library. We have settled into a routine which I find comfortable, but I miss working with children and adolescents – and having a man who shows me love. But I am content enough.

A desire to have the time to research ideas has bitten me deeply. I no longer want to return to teach a single classroom. As before during my life, I have veered away from previous ambitions to look for something new and more challenging.

The Clarendon school invited me to come back as a teacher. Though I had hoped to return to Yankton City with my librarian degree, Ms. Young was still the school's librarian. My preference was to use my new degree. But most important, Peter had just finished his first year of high school. My return to the Clarendon school was not in the cards.

Nevertheless, we could have returned. I could have taught my own class and waited for my chance for Ms. Young to leave, or, even more obviously, looked for possibilities in different towns to work as a school librarian. Penmont schools already had waiting lists of people with more experience than I, so I decided against even pursuing a school librarian job here.

Peter has taken several national tests and his results rank him in the top 1% of all children who have taken them. He has flourished these last three years, found most of his teachers to be very supportive and, perhaps due to his gregariousness, gathered a host of buddies around him he likes being with. He does not want to budge and move again.

"All my friends are here", he argued. I could not disagree. Despite the rigorous schedule he has had to deal with these last several years, he has enjoyed learning French. His pride in his ability to express himself in another language is evident daily.

Before starting high school a year ago, Peter was enthusiastic about joining the lacrosse team, playing tennis, being on the basketball team, competing in golf tournaments, running track, and wowing spectators in ping-pong. In realistic moments at the time, he knew he would have to eliminate many of those. I saw a looming conflict between staying in the French immersion program, as organized, and playing sports.

***

I am a mother. I organize my life around Peter's. I can't and don't want to do otherwise and am now taking stock of my thirty-seven years this summer. I can see that Peter will soon be more and more involved in school, sports, friends, and his own future. I have a master's degree in library science for elementary schools. There are not a whole lot of us with those credentials. Most of the existing school librarians have no master's degrees. A few have no degrees at all and got their librarian jobs after years of teaching. Statistically, they are mostly older women. I am still, comparatively, in the prime of my life, so I still have a lot of options. But when Peter graduates in three years, I will be forty, a shocking age which staggers me when I think about it.

Would anyone want to hire me at that age as an unknown? What about a man in my life? Referring to Long Jon, I have had uncertain feelings about an old friend becoming my lover. Maybe if he ever showed more interest than he has.... I have deep affection for him. That I know. He isn't the 'all-my-dreams-fulfilled' man like Walter was, but I get a comforting feeling when around him... and he is not bad looking. So, maybe it's about his feelings towards me that are in question.

I remember Ellen writing while I was still studying to be a teacher that finding a good man was "such a chore". I have that feeling now, and since I like men, I date them. All too often, though, they soon become disappointing with either drinking problems, secret drug addictions or anger-control issues. They occasionally turn out to be gay, chase other women or express shocking prejudices. All too often men also develop feelings of superiority, a need to control, or something, that undermines a healthy relationship with a woman. I could go on listing other problems, which is not to say women don't have their own negative issues. I make efforts, unsuccessfully sometimes, not to be overtly critical. I know I have that tendency.

As Ellen said back then, I'm still consciously looking – when I make time.

I know Long Jon is neither reserved nor shy, but ever since he gave me those touching compliments, he has never ventured physical affection towards me. I have begun to wonder about his private life. If Ellen knows about his preferences, I'll call them, she has never said. He gives no hint, and I'd probably never dare ask.

***

Before starting high school, Peter partly solved the schedule conflict between sports and French immersion by promising to limit himself to playing only one sport at a time, making his choice based on how often, and when, practices are required, and how often competitions take place. His decision to select a sport depending on its schedule showed he could make solid choices.

First, he ruled out ping-pong, suggesting he could quench his thirst to get accomplished by challenging our neighbor's son to games on the ping-pong table in his basement. Track happened in spring, he reminded me, but he could do a lot of practice on his own. Track meets, however, took place following classes on school days. He saw a conflict there. Golf also started in the spring, but golf competitions were generally done on weekends. That, he said, was good, but practice was done on school days and required a lot of time to get to and from the golf course.

"I haven't finished yet," he said. "There are still more sports to research," he remarked, after adding football and baseball to his list. The popular jocks were involved in the famous three: football, basketball, and baseball. Football came first in fall, then basketball in winter, followed by baseball in the spring, so they offered no schedule conflicts between them. Peter considered these. He didn't know yet how tall he might grow to be, but knew his papa was 5'-10" and I was 5'-3". From inconclusive statistical research, Peter had to accept that the eventual height of children of mixed-race couples was unpredictable. While discussing his findings, and feelings, with me, he admitted the game of football did not tempt him, nor having to wear all that "gear", and he felt no interest in "slow-moving and boring" baseball.

"My dad was a high school basketball star, wasn't he? Basketball won't conflict with many other sports since it's played inside during winter." Peter impressed me with a matrix he was preparing, and under the heading 'Practice', for basketball he wrote:

> After school, in gym. Three times a week: intensive.

Under 'Competitions', he wrote:

About ½ at home, ½ at other schools, Friday nights, but much later after school.

Despite the intense nature of basketball practice, he decided he would try to get on the team and see how it worked out. He liked the speed of Lacrosse and decided to try out for it too.

"There's no conflict between basketball and lacrosse since lacrosse starts near the beginning of spring when the basketball season is usually finished", he claimed. "And the coaches of both sports said if I'm a good enough player, I can start practice a little late".

I had predicted as much. With his matrix he decided on the two sports that were already his favorites. The research he had done only proved to him that he had had the correct premonition all along and he was rightfully satisfied with himself. I knew that the two sports and French immersion on top of the other courses would keep him a very busy lad from early winter to the end of each school year.

Peter has been very busy these last three years of high school, determined to get the most out of all his high-school experiences. He eliminated lacrosse from his palate of chosen sports after his first year, claiming it was too violent to his liking. When he became a sophomore, he replaced it by going out for track. He has stuck through basketball all along these last three years and claims to love it, though he has grown no taller than 5'-10", having reached the same height as his papa about six months ago and has shown no growth spurts since.

He has never become quite the star Walter was reported to have been. Nevertheless, I am proud of him for holding firm to his conviction to stay both with his chosen sports and the French immersion program, in which he does excel. So far, he has measured up well to the name Peter, the rock, that Walter and I gave him.

***

As in an earlier period of my life, the new year has brought a flurry of changes. It is now early 1978. Ellen is approaching sixty-six and has announced her decision to retire. We just gave her an enormous party, attended by over one hundred people including Long Jon and Ellen's daughter Pam who got married while on the commune she helped start years ago out west. She still lives there and came with her twelve-year-old daughter. Peter and I were there too. In a short speech, Ellen mentioned many by name who work in the library, thanking them for helping create the vibrantly alive community that the library offers. She also thanked those who make a particular effort to provide a haven for the homeless, who everyone knows are great users of the space.

She concluded her remarks by announcing the identity of the person she and a committee of library staff and trustees had chosen to replace her as head librarian.

"We are unanimously delighted to use this occasion to disclose her name. She is in the audience. Will Abigail Boone Rawlins please come up so that I can give you my warmest hug."

She had given me no warning or preparation at all. She did not yet know that as soon as Peter graduates after his last year, I had only just agreed by letter to return to the Clarendon school to become the new librarian when Ms. Young takes her own retirement at the end of next school year.

However, of their own accord, tears jerked from my eyes. I could hardly see as I stepped up to receive her hug, which, in a different context, would have lasted an embarrassing length of time, but at that moment felt so warm and good I almost fainted. When we turned to face the audience, applause and cheers greeted us. Mama had been so correct. Ellen Ellingsworth had always been what mama called my guardian-angel. I matched that generous thought by thinking of Ellen as my fairy-godmother.

I had been so honored by Ellen that it was difficult to tell her I could not accept the position. Instead of being upset, Ellen surprised me by saying,

"Your dedication to that school and those children back in Yankton City is another fact that makes you so special, Abigail. Though you were our first choice, we know that several others on our shortlist will be able to handle the job of head librarian. You have chosen to follow your heart. You cannot go wrong with your heart as guide."

Chapter 6

At the beginning of spring 1978, Long Jon began to visit me and Peter. At first, I was intrigued, thinking he had come to see me.

His recent promotion, he told us, did not allow him to go into the field as often as before. Still supplying talent to the Ivy League, he was now what he called "the evaluator". He could not be as innovative as formerly in this new job, which he claimed to miss "almost as much as I wish I were taller". Based on reports filed by two people doing what he used to do, it was he who gave the green light for the talent to move towards enrollment. He was now the ultimate decision-maker.

At first I was disappointed to learn he visited for reasons of business. He had been following Peter's school career. In the spring of his junior year, Peter had not yet applied for college. Aware of that, Long Jon hoped to lure him towards the Ivy League. I began to take interest. Long Jon called Peter's case "a no-brainer", by which he meant that Peter was "a natural fit", another term he used.

"What do you mean by 'a natural fit'?", I asked.

"Peter's teachers' reports, his test results, my exchanges with him, everything about him shows he is an obviously gifted student," he said. "I have seen his records that mom shared with me over the years. I have become aware that he is the very model of what my schools are looking for.

"Part of our scrutiny you might call profiling, in a negative sense, in that he has the recognizable skin, hair and facial characteristics that dominate in children of mixed negro race. He also has some indigenous traits that he obviously gets from you. In short, he is exactly what the schools I represent hope for. It is profiling, true, but for a good cause. I, like you, have focused my career on trying to level the playing field for people of color. In Peter's case, I have stepped out of the office to make you both aware of how my schools can help him, financially, by paving a career path for him."

That was quite a speech, and not altogether unexpected. The upshot was that Long Jon was there to lure Peter towards his schools, with lots of money to offer. The policies of these ivy-league schools was evidence of the affirmative action programs inaugurated by our former president from Massachusetts. "That liberal", as the rankled people in Glasstonburg used to call him, was dedicated to "leveling the playing field", as Long Jon always put it.

I was all for it and explained it to Peter, who knew about affirmative action. His reaction, like mine, was positive. Long Jon described it as "a win-win proposition". All Peter had to do was pay the application fee, fill out forms and write a motivation statement.

Informal sessions with Long Jon followed as he helped Peter steer through the paperwork. I served tea and cakes. On the second such visit, after Peter left, I felt compelled to express my pent-up impatience with Long-Jon to embarrass him with the following question:

"So, Jon, tell me about your...personal life. Why is it you have invited me over to your place in the city all these years fewer times than I can count with three fingers? You're soon going to be 38. Are you hiding someone from us that I should know about?"

He looked like he didn't expect a question like that out of the blue. He looked at me for what seemed a long time without responding. My question was not simple curiosity. I wanted Long Jon to show that he had more than a casual regard for me. I just didn't know how he felt about me. That giant, Waldo Smith, otherwise known as Tiny, once said to me that the truth, no matter how hard to accept, is worth knowing. I didn't need or want to know the truth then, but I needed to know it now. Was he attracted to me? Did he have any love Interest in me?

Finally, he said, "Why do you ask?" I decided to expose my own truth, which was that I could no longer wait for a sign from him.

"If you don't care for me that way, I've got to know so I can move on," I answered, my voice getting louder as I spoke.

"Do you mean that you care about me...that way?" he asked.

"Don't you ever wonder why I haven't found someone else!?" I surprised myself with those impatient, almost shouted, words. Having had ambiguous thoughts about any relationship with him when first becoming reacquainted with him, over the years a deep affection that I yearned to express to my dear old friend had grown in me.

Long Jon released a long sigh that sounded almost like relief and sat down again. He looked at me, visibly relaxing, tension fading from around his eyes, his face shining like a full moon. He then admitted that he had suffered so many jibes as a teenager about his height that he had developed an inferiority complex. He had been involved with a coed at NYU, then with another woman several years after his graduation from that school. He had convinced himself that both women rejected him for being short.

"I was truly in love with the second woman, but she left me for a man over six feet tall. I always assumed she wanted a taller man. Thereafter, I taught myself never to show a woman how I felt, not wanting to be hurt again. Keeping my vulnerability inside was the only way I could protect my ego."

"You haven't answered my question, Jon. Do you have any special feelings for me?", I asked, too loudly and a bit impatiently. I had started this exchange but had not yet gotten satisfaction. He had not committed to answering, but we were getting closer to the truth. I felt that the ice was melting.

"Only that I have always secretly loved you, even before my family and I left Glasstonburg. You already had a boyfriend, and I was leaving, so I decided to swallow my emotions and live with them alone."

He said those words slowly and haltingly, but after saying he "always secretly loved" me, I had to hold myself back while he finished talking to encircle him with my arms, press my lips against his and show in a gentle, lingering kiss, how I felt about him. Tears beginning to show around his eyes, he responded by repeating "I've always loved you" so many times I got the impression he was expressing what had been inside for many years and he was making up for lost time.

At that moment I remembered when mama said that Mr. Jones "swept me off my feet." I loved that feeling. I hadn't felt that way since meeting Walter, so now I just gave into it. Confronting Long Jon had turned into a rediscovery of a man I thought I knew. When the kiss ended, I knew it was a new beginning for both of us.

Relaxing into the reverie of the moment we felt no need at first to talk. We gazed at one another like two adolescents who have tumbled into puppy love for the first time. After hugging, kissing, and stretching out in a reclined embrace, we simultaneously broke our long silence, each blurting out that learning the truth about how we felt about each other was liberating and magical.

Eventually, Long Jon brought our talk around to something more practical that loomed over us.

"You have committed to leaving to go back to Yankton City in less than fifteen months. I don't want to lose you now that we've shown how we feel about each other. My life feels changed forever, knowing you love me. I never knew I could feel this light and carefree…. I don't ever want to go back to the dead feeling I had before. Should I quit my job? Right now, I see that as a definite possibility because I want to stay with you. What a surprise you are, so unexpected, so…"

I had to interrupt him, if only because the happy tears running down my cheeks were getting into my mouth. He had been less prepared than I for the wonderful change that had just happened between us. After swallowing, I broke into his words.

"I want to find a way for us to be together without you having to leave your work for the universities. You mustn't think you need to quit that job. It's your very identity. You are helping the world. I can think of several alternatives for you. For one, you felt more creative in your former role discovering the talent, as you always say. You could investigate the chances of going back to that role working in the field. We have fifteen wonderful months ahead of us that give us time to come up with other possible ideas to discuss and think about".

I could feel Long Jon relaxing beside me. He muttered acknowledgement, and we decided to resume sitting up on the couch but had no wish or thought to part company. Long Jon said nothing further, keeping one arm around me. My mind was newly open to freely associate ideas, thoughts and feelings welling up inside. Just as Long Jon had brought up a practical matter that we eventually would have to deal with, my dream-like thoughts began to dissipate and, in my new awareness, I wanted to confront him with certain concerns of my own.

I began with the following words:

"I know these are serious thoughts Jon, but I have been living with them. I believe, I know, you and I will find happiness together, but you've got to share in my constant worries about my son if we are to become a couple. Allow me a few more words to get these concerns off my chest.

"We live in a strange country. You are opening the door for Peter to get into one of the best universities in the world, offering generous scholarships and a bright future, while that same boy must be careful not to be pulled over by the police while driving or even walking down the street. All that because he is black. He used to have a motor scooter that he'd bought to make the trips to classes more enjoyable. While trying to get it started one night to get home from a friend's, he got arrested for trying to steal his own scooter! The police asked no questions. They clubbed him over the head before he could even speak, and while he was still unconscious, took him to jail. I had to come and bail him out. After he showed the papers proving he was the owner, he got no apologies. The sergeant in charge only said he had looked suspicious. When I said back, 'You mean he looked black!', the sergeant only made a face and never answered.

"Since then, Peter has occasionally driven my car. He has been stopped twice so far this year by different traffic policemen asking for his ID. His last run-in with the law happened walking home from a late-night movie, right here in Penmont. He got arrested, taken to jail, and booked for jaywalking when he was only two feet off the curb, on a small, deserted street with no cars around. Such things would never have happened, I'm certain, if he had been white.

"You remember I always talked a lot, only now I talk better with a broader vocabulary. I gradually came to understand the world around me as I changed. There were things said to me back then that I just didn't grasp. Now, I understand how much our society must improve.

"I'd like to finish with one more thought I had recently that will summarize what goes on in my head. I'm referring to the Latin expressions de jure and de facto.

"De facto refers to what happens 'in fact', on the ground, or in my opinion in this context, within the minds of individuals. We can't control what people think, like the way those cops who arrested my son saw him. However, we can control what they do through de jure, 'by law', to fight back. Law was used to create segregation. I've seen examples of it in several places, including the example my former husband Walter detailed for me once of Ironside Tract where his family lived close to Yankton City. If racial segregation was created de jure, then we can get rid of it de jure. To bring sundown to racial segregation, we need to focus on passing, and enforcing, laws that have enough bite to control what people do. My hope is that de jure will someday help lower the power of de facto".

"I would feel proud to have thought of what you just said," Long Jon concluded as I nestled my cheek against his neck. Our doubts concerning each other had just met their final sundown, put to rest before greeting a new sunrise.

THE END

NAMED PEOPLE, THINGS, AND PLACES
(In order of appearance or reference in the story)

Abigail Boone – Protagonist: variously also known as *Nig, Gabi* & *Abi*

Jasmine – Abigail's mother, married to Mr. Jones

Big Mama – Abigail's Cherokee grandma, named Elohi

Tadpole – Abigail's 1st boyfriend she calls *Tad*, but his real name is Larry LaPierre.

Mrs. Wesley – Married name of Ellen Ellingsworth, neighbor who teaches Abigail grammar and spelling.

Glasstonburg – Northern town where Abigail lives.

Mr. Jones – Abigail's stepfather who some call "Sod"

Mother Jones – (by reference only) Mr. Jones' deceased first wife.

Grandpapa – Grandfather of the Jones children who offers nickels for dead rats.

Milk Brothers – Nickname of the two oldest Jones boys, also sometimes called *'sons of Sod'*.

Moon Boy – Nickname of Billie Jones, Abigail's younger stepbrother.

Jer – Jerry Jones, oldest of Abigail's stepbrothers

The Menace – Dennis Jones, five-year-old younger brother of Jer and Moon Boy.

Knuckle – Nickname her brother gave Margie Jones.

Brain – Nickname her brother gave Mercy Jones.

Tar Heels – True term for North Carolinians, used pejoratively by some in Glasstonburg for Abigail and her mother.

Gyro Gearloose – Pejorative nickname for Patrick, boy in the city dump

Long Jon – Nickname for Jonathan Wesley, son of Mrs. Wesley

Pam – Pamela, daughter of Mrs. Wesley.

City-limit Road – Runs in front of the Wesley house.

Trench Road – Runs by Wesley house to City-limit Road.

Uncle – Nickname of Ronnie who lives up Trench Road.

Old Maid – Nickname used for Mabel behind her back; she eats ice cream and chats with Abigail in the ice-cream shop.

Elvis – (Real person): Elvis Presley

Possum – Known to Abigail in high school. She does not know his real name. He played on the basketball team.

Cliff – Clifford Drum, Abigail's second boyfriend

Langford – Father of Clifford Drum

'Drum and Dobro' – Name Langford Drum gave his guitar act.

Mr. Niles – The 'passer' who hid, while alive, from the entire town of Glasstonburg that he was a 'negro'.

Pea-Dad Cunningham – friend of Long Jon's from high school. Abigail knows only his last name and nickname.

Big Apple – Real nickname for New York City.

Yankton City – Town 12 miles from Glasstonburg where Abigail goes to live and attend teacher's college.

Clarendon Foundation – It funded construction of the school where Abigail teaches.

Agnes Short – Abigail's neighbor in the apartment building in Yankton City.

Reginald Steffens – Owner of the apartment building where Abigail lives in Yankton City. He becomes her good friend.
Midtown Apartments – Name of Reginald's apartment house.
Walter Rawlins – Abigail's husband and great love.
South Hope – Town where Walter Rawlins lived before marriage to Abigail.
Hope – Town north of South Hope. (Reference only)
Ironside Tract – Subdivision in South Hope where Walter's family lives.
My Motto – Real poem by Langston Hughes.
Brer Rabbit – Real character in *Uncle Remus* stories.
Little Buddha – Name Abigail and Walter use for their son just after his birth.
Waldo Smith – Nicknamed *Tiny* by his mates; Walter recruited him into the army to be an 'advisor' in Viet Nam.
Peter – Name given by Abigail and Walter to their son.
Roger – Boy in Abigail's classroom first year.
Willie – Boy in Abigail's classroom first year.
Randy – Boy in Abigail's classroom
Debra – Girl in Abigail's classroom
Sandra – Girl in Abigail's classroom
President Johnson – Lyndon Baines Johnson, real U.S. president.
General Westmoreland – real general in Vietnam
Penmont, New York – Suburb of New York City where Ellen Ellingsworth moves after Glasstonburg to live with her parents.

Made in the USA
Columbia, SC
22 October 2023